What readers are saying

"Liz Adams' *Alice's Sexual Discovery* is an exciting new erotic twist on the old fairytale. As you follow Alice through her journey, you will find yourself slipping into her delectable fantasies. The descriptions involve all of your senses, letting you feel each teasing touch, taste every musky man, and smell the steam of sex. Just when you think Alice is done teasing you, a new scenario pops up that will leave you craving more. I highly recommend that you take a journey and lose yourself in the passionate wonderland you never knew existed...until now."
~ **Rebecca Hoffman, editor with Grit City Publications and author of *Drop in the Ocean*:**
http://rebeccamhoffman.blogspot.com

"I have to confess I always thought Alice in Wonderland was a bit stupid. It didn't quite captivate me and I figured my imagination just wasn't that obscure. The same however can't be said for Liz Adam's wonderfully creative erotic rewrite. Right from the moment Alice falls down the hole we realize this is a very different – yet similar – Wonderland. It helps to have read the original because it's just wonderful to see how Adam's has re-imagined the characters and events. A rabbit? Sure, but it's the name of a deliciously cute naked man. Off with their heads? Absolutely...but not the heads the original queen was after. Overall? This is deliciously wicked. Have a man or a vibrator with you when you read it."

~ **Simone Sinna, erotic-romance suspense author of** *Embedded* **and** *Exposé:* **www.simonesinna.com**

"I loved this book. I read it almost all in one go. The story pulls you in and won't let you leave, very much like Alice's experience between the pages. Every scene is deliciously sensual as you follow Alice on an adventure to find what's eluding her. Even when some of the encounters are as strange as events in the original, they are so naughty and outrageous you can't help but be turned on by them. Liz Adams has created a fantastical world where anything can happen and her characters are so vividly drawn you really feel as though you are in the story. She keeps you on a knife edge right to the very end, just like Alice. Liz is a brilliant storyteller and her words flow effortlessly across the page. I promise you, you won't be able to put it down."

~ **Lexie Bay, author of** *Inside Looking Out:* **http://lexiebay.co.uk**

"A wild, erotic ride through the scenes of the book's namesake, complete with all the characters, but in x-rated versions. A sexy adventure for Alice, ending in a completely romantic happily-ever-after. Erotic fantasy readers will love this book."

~ **Randi Alexander, Author of** *Rode Hard and Put Up Satisfied:* **http://RandiAlexander.com**

"Ms Adams has truly changed the way we look at fairy tales in this erotic tale that introduces you to the new rabbit hole! I look forward to more erotic tales from this talented author."

~ **Tonya Kinzer, Author of** *The Boss's Pet* **series: http://www.tonyakinzer.com**

"Liz has written a story that blows your mind. With lots of sloppy fingers, Alice's clit throbs for attention from the naked buff men she meets along the way. With tongues that make Alice flood the world with her sweet elixir. Wow! In between that, the swallowing, chewing and licking certain types of...um body parts. Alice grows or shrinks to help her reach the perfect orgasm erotic style. With continual prodding and poking throughout the book, in search for sexual arousal. You're going to wish you had a dress like Alice's that will take you to Wonderland and back. So the whimpers will escape your lips."

~ **Melissa Craig, author of *Plentiful Package:***
http://www.melissacraigauthor.wordpress.com

ALICE'S SEXUAL DISCOVERY IN A WONDERFUL LAND

Alice's Erotic Adventures

Book 1

LIZ ADAMS

ALICE'S SEXUAL DISCOVERY IN A WONDERFUL LAND
(ALICE'S EROTIC ADVENTURES, BOOK 1)

Published by: Barany Publishing
ISBN-13: 978-0-9895004-9-4

.

Author's Note

I found writing this erotic version of *Alice's Adventures in Wonderland* more challenging than I had anticipated. Wanting to stay true to the original story, I noticed that Alice never stayed with one character long enough to build a meaningful relationship. As a result, in this erotic version, she ends up traveling from character to character having sexual encounters with each one. If you prefer erotic romance, I'm afraid you'll be greatly disappointed. But if you're looking for a fun frolic in Alice's wonderland with many of the familiar characters, this will be just your cup of tea!

Just a heads up. You'll notice that Tweedle Dee and Tweedle Dum don't make an appearance. That's because they are in *Alice Through the Looking Glass* and not in *Alice's Adventures in Wonderland*. I have also left out the Mock Turtle scene since turtles have the tendency to slow down the pacing (heh, heh).

ALICE'S SEXUAL

DISCOVERY

IN A

WONDERFUL LAND

Alice's Erotic Adventures

Book 1

Chapter 1

NIGHT'S promise of the forbidden blanketed across the sky, seeking to penetrate the windows of Alice's manor. Alice stood at the second-story window brushing her long hair. She was glad to be back from Newnham, that all-girls college in Cambridge University. Getting away from all those giggles and high voices was a welcome relief. So was coming home to see the stars shining above the manor she grew up in. Being home for the holidays, Alice could sleep in, read what she wanted, go to the cinema, and just relax. Tomorrow she'd call all her friends from secondary school.

What was that outside? Something moved in the garden, but it was hard to tell what. With the lights on in her room and the darkness outside, Alice had to rely on the moonlight to reveal the midnight motion. She squinted. It was Jack. Her heart sped up.

Jack had been the gardener for Alice's family since Alice was fifteen, and he was only a few years Alice's senior. That made him now twenty-two?

He was, oh, so cute with his scruff of short, black hair above his gorgeous eyes and chiseled chin.

When she was fifteen, it had taken her months to get bold enough to go beyond "Hi," and actually try to have a conversation with him.

Alice remembered that day she finally spoke to him. She and her sister Lois had just come back from seeing a Beatles film.

Jack had been tending to the tomato bushes. He was shirtless, his glistening muscles rippled in the sun.

Alice swallowed. "I just saw 'A Hard Day's Night!' "

Jack stood up straight and looked at Alice. Lord, those blue eyes!

"That new Beatles film." He wiped his hands on his jeans. His voice had a slight growl that was sexy as hell. "Ever since I met you, you've raved about them. Big fan, eh?"

Alice nodded emphatically. "Big fan!"

"I'm more of a jazz guy, myself. But I can't say I blame you. The Beatles are pretty damn good. How'd you like the movie?"

"It was really good! All the songs. They're incredible!"

"Great. I must see it some time." Jack squinted at Alice. "How was the popcorn?"

"Uh…good. How did you know I…?"

"You've got a small piece there near your lips. Here. Hold still."

Alice didn't move. Jack placed a finger on her and stroked her lower lip. The feeling of his tender finger across her lip shot jolts through her body.

"There." He smiled at her. "Now no one else will know."

Was it Alice's imagination or were their eyes locked longer than usual? Jack cleared his throat, muttered something about the tomatoes, and returned to tending the plants.

Alice sighed and watched him pull off the dry leaves. He seemed to actually like what he was doing.

There must be some way to keep the conversation going. She toed the earth. "What made you want to be a gardener?"

Jack looked up at Alice. Alice thought she could spend all day looking into his blue eyes.

He smiled. "Thank you."

What was he thanking her for? She giggled. *Stupid giggle!*

"No one's ever asked me that before," he explained. "When I think of how I'm able to help a seed grow into all of nature's colors just by giving it the love and attention it needs, it makes me feel so…alive."

Did he just say "love?" How many boys did she know could say the word "love" without sounding like they were trying on a dress? None. Jack said "love" like it was the most comfortable part of his life. He conveyed his feelings with such ease.

"And the results of my affection," Jack plucked a red tomato from the bush, "taste incredible."

He held the red fruit to Alice's lips. She closed her eyes and bit into the warm fruit, tasting in its juices Jack's love and affection.

She opened her eyes. There were his baby blues. Alice lost herself in them.

She stopped herself from saying "I love you," and giggled instead.

Jack turned away. He picked off the dead leaves on the plant in front of him, and without looking at Alice, he said, "You're a good friend. A sweet, little girl."

Alice choked. *A sweet, little girl? As in "I-love-you-like-a-sister sweet, little girl"?* That's when it hit her. Jack would never love her. *Really* love her. She wasn't pretty enough. She was just a sweet, little girl. Not beautiful, not attractive. Probably loved his stupid plants more than her. *Damn! Damn! Damn!*

"Is something wrong?" Jack asked.

"What? No! Nothing! I just got some dirt…" Choking on her words, Alice wiped her eyes and ran off.

That painful realization was the best thing for her, as far as Alice was concerned. At least she knew how Jack felt. Knowing she could never be in a relationship with him was better than not knowing how he felt. She was able to get on with her life. Over the years she even flirted with Jack. Flirting came easy knowing that nothing she said could ruin the chance of them being together. Because there *was* no chance of them being together. They were just friends. Jack had made that quite clear.

She had spent the next few years convincing herself there were other men out in the world. And when she went to university, Alice knew she'd have the opportunity to admire many young men in the nearby coed colleges in Cambridge.

But after coming home from those first several months at university, right in front of her was Jack passing through the garden in the middle of the night and she couldn't deny how her heart still sped up at the shadowy sight of him. It looked as though Jack might be noticing her standing at the window.

She reached with her free hand to caress her breast through the soft fabric of her silk nightgown. Such a bold action, it surprised even her that she was doing it. She lifted her head back as though relishing the sensation. With her eyes half-closed she kept an eye on Jack.

Yes. He was still looking at her. Knowing he was watching her made her pulse quicken. But she then realized the consequence of her game. What had she done? Their relationship was now going to completely change, and there was no way to undo her hand-on-breast stunt.

If you're going to play, as her classmates would often tell her, *play all the way!*

Alice pretended not to notice as she placed the hairbrush on the table beside her and used both hands to massage her chest.

Am I a sweet little girl now, Jack? Is this what sweet girls do? Do these look like they belong to a little girl? Her hands squeezed and tweaked creating familiar sensations among an all too unfamiliar audience. *I am not a sweet little girl. No way. Are you watching me Jack? Are you seeing me?*

Alice breathed hard. She peeked. He was watching her. And maybe, just maybe, he was seeing her, too.

Her nipples hardened. She wanted to touch them directly, but Alice was afraid that if she stopped what she was doing, even to take off her nightgown, it would scare Jack off. So she continued to press her breasts, squeeze them, pet them. Anything to make this moment last as long as possible.

She thought about what Jack was seeing. *Was he hard? Was he turned on?* But perhaps the more important question was, did he like her body?

Alice panted. *Lord, was his breathing as heavy as*

mine? She pictured Jack touching her, caressing her breasts, pinching her nipples, telling her how stunning she was, how he'd always loved her and had always wanted her forever.

Alice peeked again. Oh! Unless her eyes deceived her, Jack had his hand down his pants! He was actually turned on by what she was doing!

She wondered what his cock looked like. Or, for that matter, what any cock looked like. Alice had never seen one before. One time, her older sister's friend Carol had described one to her at Alice's insistence. But even Carol's description wasn't very helpful. Alice bet Jack's was big and hard.

This is for you, Jack. Only for you.

Alice wanted to feel him, entering her, pushing into her, thrusting through her, holding her in his arms.

She'd never had a boyfriend and wanted Jack more than any man she ever knew.

Especially now. Because right now she needed someone inside her.

Moving a hand down the front of her chest, to her belly, to her thigh, she made sure to glide her hand down her body slowly and not frighten Jack away. She knew that if she moved too quickly, he may think the show's over and leave. A smile slipped across her face. She realized that moving slowly would not only maintain the illusion that she wasn't stopping anytime soon, but also be as sexy as hell to Jack.

Curiosity overcame her and she peeked at him again. He was still there. His arm was moving up and down in his pants. She imagined that strong hand stroking himself.

With her own seductive hand, she inched up her nightgown and placed a bare foot on the low window ledge. Lots of leg had to be showing through the window, to Jack. She moved her hands between her thighs and separated the folds with a finger, feeling herself open to the window, to the garden, to Jack. It must have been a surprise for him, because his arm was moving faster now as though he were desperately pumping the well for water. Alice let a finger dip inside of her, imagining it was Jack's beautiful shaft filling her. She felt her wetness.

It wasn't enough.

Keeping a finger stimulating her clit, she slowly reached for her hairbrush. She reversed the hairbrush and put the tip of the handle to her pussy.

Do you like this, Jack? Do you like what you're seeing?

Alice daydreamed he liked it very much, indeed. That it was him inching into her at this very moment.

"I love you, Alice," he was saying. "I love you so much."

He went in deeper. Filling her.

Alice clutched her breast, felt the handle of the brush open her. Moving it out felt just as good.

She checked. Jack was still there gazing up at her.

She felt so big above him as he stroked his gorgeous cock for her.

And it was for her.

She moved the handle faster, letting it touch her deep inside. Faster. Having it be Jack. He was pushing into her. Faster. Jack thrusting his cock inside of her.

Alice moaned. She loved being watched by him.

Could this be the moment? Could this be the night she found out what an orgasm feels like? Even without a real cock inside her?

She put all her attention on rubbing her clit, feeling the brush handle inside of her. *Forget about Jack,* she told herself, *and just focus on achieving the big O. Focus on the climax. Focus on the climax.*

But the faster she rubbed and thrust the hairbrush inside of her, the further from that peak she felt. She slowed down her efforts. As usual, it wasn't going to happen.

Was Jack still watching?

She opened her eyes to look at him directly.

Jack froze, then turned away. In a flash, he disappeared into the shadows.

The moment was gone.

Dammit! Why did I look at him so brazenly?

But Alice was thrilled. She had connected with Jack in a wonderful and new way. Was it really possible? Could Jack fall for her, after all? How was this going to play out tomorrow? What would it be like talking to him? Would he ignore her? Would he stare at her with a knowing smile? Would he stutter every time he tried to talk to her? Would she end up the stutterer and spit out another stupid giggle like she had so many years ago?

She released a delightful sigh and tossed the tired, moistened hairbrush on the table. After turning off the lights she fell backwards onto her bed laughing. What a problem she created for herself! Such an exquisite problem! Just when she thought there wasn't any chance of Jack being attracted to her, her entire world changed. She snuggled under the covers and tried to go to sleep, but couldn't put it out of her mind. Hours would go by before she fell asleep.

ALICE lay in bed feeling a need to be touched. Cupping her hand between her legs, she massaged her nub with a determined finger. She'd made a connection with Jack unlike ever before. This time, she was certain that memory could help her reach orgasm. She could finally know what it'd be like to come.

Her fingers rubbed harder, faster, worrying her clit. It felt good but she wasn't getting any higher. What was wrong with her?

There was a noise at the door. The door opened

and Jack strolled into her darkened bedroom.

Alice stopped moving her hand. What was he doing in her room? The better question was, what was he going to do with her in her room?

Jack ignored her. He went to the window and looked out just as she had done. The moonlight revealed his stern face.

Since Alice's hand was under the covers and the room was so dark, she figured she could keep moving without Jack noticing.

Here he was in her bedroom. A dream come true.

With Alice's other hand she discreetly slipped two fingers inside of her. She probed herself deeply trying to find that elusive climax. She thrummed and twirled at her impatient yet stubborn clit.

Jack turned to her. Was that repulsion in his face?

Alice continued her fervent mission, her hands shaking visibly underneath the sheets.

Jack pointed an angry finger at her. "You don't know a thing about how to please a man, do you? Why I bet you wouldn't know what to do with a cock if one were in front of your face."

Alice worked harder, grinding her hips against her hands, hungry for satisfaction and only getting hungrier.

"Look at you," Jack sneered. "You can't even have an orgasm. Why would any man bother with you?"

Alice woke up in a sweat. She found herself needing to catch her breath.

She looked around the bedroom. Her hairbrush still glistened from her juices in the moonlight. But Jack being inside her room? That was just a nightmare.

No, not just a nightmare. It was the truth.

Chapter 2

A LICE and her sister's friend Carol sat outside
the manor in the back garden by the lake. They
had parked themselves under the shade of an oak tree
whose leaves painted a pointillist display of sun dots
on the earth. The two of them were separated from
the lake by a well-trimmed meadow. A constant cool
breeze blew against them. Alice supposed Carol's
sundress struggled to keep Carol warm, as much as
Alice's own blue dress and white apron rippled and
fought the breeze.

"Have you ever had an orgasm?" Alice asked her
sister's friend.

"Alice!" Carol laughed and plopped the history
book down in her lap causing a subtle breeze to blow

against the grass they sat in. Carol straightened her beautiful orange dress over her ankles, though it truly did not seem to need any straightening at all.

True, Alice's choice of question to change the subject was not the most polite one, but listening to Carol read a history lesson to prepare for an exam was as exciting as watching the trees race to see which would be the first to grow the tallest.

"Honestly, Carol. Now that we're on Christmas break from university, I don't want to listen to your stupid history book."

"Alice, your sister may be a wiz at Victorian history, but right now I need a study partner if I want to even *hope* to pass. And since Lois is off with your parents going shopping, you have the honor of being my study partner until they return."

"That's another thing," Alice said. "You've been spending so much time here that I've probably seen more of you than your parents have. I mean, I know Lois is your best friend and all that, but don't you think your ma and pa are missing you?"

"My mother and father are on their own Christmas vacation in France. Let them have their fun. Besides, I wouldn't want you to miss the privilege of my precious company. Now back to my Victorian history book."

Alice grabbed the book out of Carol's hands and placed it far out of Carol's reach.

"Fine." Carol shrugged. "I'll just have to wait

until Lois returns to help me study."

"So, have you?"

"Have I what?" Carol tucked her long, brown hair behind her ears.

Alice just grinned. It took Carol some time to notice Alice's smirk.

"Alice!" Carol looked shocked.

"Well?"

"Yes." Carol blushed.

Alice froze. She couldn't believe her ears. "You have?"

"Of course. Haven't you?"

Alice let her gaze fall on the history book beside her and scratched an itch at her neck.

"You haven't?!"

"Shh!" Alice glanced around. But there was no reason to fear someone overhearing. "It's not like I haven't tried."

"I know."

Alice scowled. "What do you mean, 'you know'?"

"Last night, as I passed your room, I heard panting."

"You heard me?"

"Loud and clear."

Alice caught herself from showing any signs that would admit something happened. She slowly leaned back against the tree and said, "That doesn't mean anything. Maybe I just finished running in circles around the room, or maybe I had insomnia and was trying to force myself to pass out by hyperventilating."

Carol laughed. "I cracked open the door and saw you standing at the window with your nightgown hiked up, stuffing the handle of your hairbrush—"

"Okay! Okay! Geez!" Alice felt her ears grow hot. "I didn't know anyone was watching me." *Anyone except Jack, that is.*

Carol didn't have a clue about what really happened last night. Alice doubted Carol had ever experienced something as exciting as being watched in her life.

And yet, she said she's been able to orgasm. Alice remembered what Jack had said in her dream. *You can't even have an orgasm. Why would any man bother with you?* Why, indeed. If she couldn't come during sex, her man might lose interest in the bedroom and, eventually, lose interest in her. Faking orgasm was always a solution, but Alice didn't think a bedroom of lies was great for a relationship. No. If she wanted to have a satisfying relationship, be it with Jack or another hunk in her future, then knowing how to reach the big O was necessary.

"How do you do it?" Alice said aloud.

"How do I do what?" Carol reached over Alice to retrieve her history book.

"You know, reach orgasm?"

Carol laughed.

"I mean—" Alice felt her cheeks redden. "Can you do it just by touching yourself?"

"Yes," Carol smiled like the cat that drank the cream, ate the pie, went to the pub and got smashed.

Alice couldn't believe it. She figured that to get herself to come, she would have to wait until she actually had a real live cock thrusting in and out of her. Save that, and an orgasm would never happen. Was there actually a secret to it? The way to touch yourself? The places to touch? Some sort of proper order?

"Show me," Alice said.

"What?" Carol sounded shocked.

Alice didn't care. "Show me how you touch yourself to orgasm."

"I will not!" Carol said, but she was smirking.

"Why not? You got to see me touch myself."

Carol laughed. "Oh right. Like *that's* a good reason."

"Please! I've never had one. I must be doing something wrong."

"You didn't seem to be doing anything wrong last night. And what about this?" Carol reached over to Alice's dress pocket, patting the book Alice kept there. "Doesn't that saucy book of yours help?"

How did she know I've been reading The Story of O? Alice put her hand over the pocket, feeling the book underneath, as though covering it with her hand would somehow help hide it from Carol.

"Honestly, Alice," Carol laughed. "If that doesn't make you orgasm, nothing will."

Alice didn't say anything. She just gritted her teeth. That really hurt. As if no matter what she did, no matter how she stimulated herself, she'd never experience what normal people experienced. Just like her dream. *You can't even have an orgasm. Why would any man bother with you?* Alice leaned back against the tree and bit back the tears Carol didn't deserve to see.

"What?" Carol softened her voice. "What's wrong?"

Alice said nothing.

"I was just kidding."

The breeze continued to blow against them. Her vision blurred.

"I'm sorry if I hurt you," Carol said searching Alice's face. "Alice?"

Alice said nothing. The wind rustled through the long grass. In the distance, the farm animals grunted, shrieked, and lowed.

"Alice, I'm sorry."

"Forget it."

Carol caressed Alice's cheek, but Alice turned away. She supposed it was stupid to be upset over something as silly as not being able to come. Why was she so upset over it? But that wasn't it. That wasn't what upset her.

The tiny door to the truth was opening. A door that revealed how Alice was a freak.

She had to come to terms with it. Could Jack ever love a freak?

The truth sliced her heart. Jack couldn't. No one could. That was the reality, wasn't it?

Alice felt like the smallest, most insignificant soul on Earth. She turned her head away so Carol wouldn't see the stinging wetness in her eyes.

"Okay." Carol leaned back against the tree, working to get comfortable. She wagged a finger at Alice, "But don't you tell a soul about this, or I'll murder you!"

Alice wiped her eyes. "Forget it. Nothing can help me."

"Alice, just shut up and watch what I do, okay?"

Alice sat unbelieving as Carol pulled up her own skirt.

"You're really going to do it?"

"Not. A. Soul."

"Not a soul," Alice crossed her heart and spit on the ground. "I promise!"

Carol scooted against the tree and leaned her head back. "Okay then." She closed her eyes and bent her knees to bring her feet closer, adjusted the hem of her dress to her waist to bare her legs. Alice watched Carol open her legs. Carol touched the inside of her thighs with one hand and stroked the outside of her panties with the other.

Alice wondered if bypassing the breasts was the trick. It didn't make sense.

Alice looked at Carol's face. Her eyes were still closed and she had a peaceful look about her. What was she thinking about? Was she thinking about a sordid experience she had that Alice didn't know about? Was she thinking about a certain guy?

Carol slipped a hand down her panties, her fingers caressing beneath.

It had to be a guy. But who?

Something caught Alice's eye. She looked up and noticed that Jack was standing at a distance, frozen in his tracks, his eyes glued to Carol's task.

And he was hot!

He must have been working in the garden because all he wore were pants held up by suspenders. His bare chest was slick with sweat, and his muscles bulged in all their glory.

They didn't look like the only thing bulging.

Alice knew she should jostle Carol and stop her. Alice had promised she wouldn't tell a soul.

Carol's breathing got heavier.

Maybe Carol would never know he watched her. It was probably better that way. It was probably better that she never know than realize she'd been caught.

Carol's face stiffened and contorted like it was puzzling over something. Her breaths deepened and got louder.

Best not to tell her. After all, Alice wasn't actually saying anything to anyone. She was still true to her word.

Carol's hand flattened, her fingertips moving

rapidly under her panties. Her other hand squeezed a breast, kneading it.

Alice squirmed and glanced at Jack. He kept his eyes on Carol from where he stood tall and majestic like a Greek statue.

Alice's heart leapt. He was beautiful.

Then she turned back to Carol. Carol moaned softly.

Who was Carol thinking of that made her so excited?

Then Alice felt like an idiot. Of course it was Jack. Carol had visited Lois throughout Alice's childhood, and Jack was the only man around. The only gorgeous man, anyway. And look at her. Look at Carol. She was prettier than Alice.

No. Not just prettier. She was beautiful. Those Caribbean-colored eyes surrounded by a shoulder-length flip of ginger hair. That petit nose barely noticeable above her princess smile, full lips revealing a brilliant set of sexy teeth.

But what about last night? He seemed hot and bothered by my show at the window. He is attracted to me, right?

None of that mattered. As long as Carol was the prettier one, Jack would never go after Alice. And even if he did. Even if, for some reason, he gave Alice a chance, he'd find out how much of a dunce Alice was as a sex partner, and he'd drop her like a rotten fruit.

Jack leaned on his rake, his ribbed abdomen breathing deeply. He loved Carol. Not Alice.

When Alice looked at Carol, she knew exactly what Carol was thinking. That was Jack's chest she was leaning back on. That was Jack's hand caressing her breast through the dress. Those were Jack's fingers rubbing her clit.

Alice saw red. She stood up and stormed away.

Let them have their stupid moment. Jack doesn't care about me, that's just fine.

Did Carol, that damned woman, even notice Alice had left her alone? Alice turned to look behind her as she kept walking away.

And fell down a hole.

Chapter 3

THE drop hurt like hell.

Alice landed on a patch of roots and dirt. She clutched the tender part of her waist that had hit a large tree root. There would be a bruise there for days. Standing up in this dark area, she took a damage report, patting herself down. A bruised hip and a bit of a scratched hand. Her dress was dirty, but had survived the fall. She straightened her hair.

Where was she? The dirty brick walls were just a dark, hollow cylinder straight up. Alice knew this place. It was the estate's old well, forgotten and left for nature to reclaim.

Something moved on the walls. She froze. If she didn't know any better she'd say it was a naked man that went through an imperceptible doorway. *A man down here? It made no sense.*

Alice reached out to find the wall and feel if it led to a doorway. Her hands landed on skin.

"Oh!" She yanked back her hands. "Sorry!"

She waited for a response, but there was none. Was there really someone there? Instead of reaching her hands out again, she shifted closer, ready to delicately nudge against whatever or whoever it was with her shoulder. She connected, and felt his fingers graze across her arm. She stepped back.

"Who's there?"

Silence. Whoever it was didn't come after her. As though stepping into the center of the well was her safe zone.

Alice slowly stepped back into his vicinity. Delicate fingers touched her arm once more. She shivered. Her breaths came, uneven. He – it had to be a man even though she couldn't see him – was exciting her with the gentlest of touches.

What would Jack say if he found out Alice let herself be touched by a stranger? Would he be jealous? Would he be angry? Alice could see him now getting red in the face. Alice smiled and stepped closer to the groping hands.

Desiring to be a little more passive, she turned away from him. Powerful muscular hands massaged her shoulders. Alice dropped her head forward and let his strong fingers push out the tension inside her. His oh-so-good hands swept down her back toward her waist.

Where else would his fingers touch her? How far would she let this anonymous man go?

This is a dangerous game, Alice, she told herself.

But, oh, it felt so good! Alice's nipples hardened. Would their desire for his touch be fulfilled? Surely he wouldn't go that far. But Alice did indeed feel his warm hands reach her waist and inch upwards along her sides. She shivered. She never knew she was so sensitive there.

She knew where those confident hands were going.

She should run, shouldn't she? That's what Lois and Carol would say. And Jack. Out of jealousy?

She ignored the voices and let herself lean back against him. His chest was warm and solid against her back. His hardness fit against her, nestling against the crevice of her bottom.

Then his hands were upon her breasts. He held them so gently, as if her breasts were a precious exotic fruit. A hand loving her left. A hand rolling her right. A hand reaching between her legs... *Three hands?!*

Alice screamed. She jumped from the hands and ran to the opposite wall of the well. The wall had an opening to a small cave. She blindly followed the path of the cave, anything to get as far away from those hands as possible. Up ahead was a curve of the cave and a light. She followed the glow into a long, bright hallway. Alice squinted.

Where the hell am I?

Dozens of doors were alongside each wall. The hallway looked immaculate. The walls were white, the doors were white. The most curious thing of all had to be how bright everything was. And not a single light bulb anywhere!

She tried a few of the doors, rattled them. All locked. She hustled forward until she came upon a coffee table in the middle of the hallway. A key lay upon it, a tiny key. It clearly wouldn't fit any of the keyholes. Then she saw the tiny door by her ankles. No way she could fit through that portal.

Along the hallway of doors was something else – or someone – Alice hadn't noticed before. On the lower part of the wall, hanging upside down from chains, was a tiny, bearded man without a stitch of clothing on. He was so small! He looked more like a large doll than a man. Was he even real? If he was a doll, he was the most realistic-looking one Alice had ever seen.

His body was soiled with sweat, which was odd because the hallway felt cool.

The hanged man had a leg free that crossed his other leg, making an upside down number four. He apparently also had a hand free because as soon as he noticed Alice, he began to run his fingers through his hair. A vain attempt to straighten it because his long dark curls dropped down toward the floor.

Alice approached and noticed the man was about

half her height. So very strange!

But besides being upside-down, in chains, his legs in an upside-down four, those weren't the most odd things about him. The most prominent thing about him was his cock.

So this was a man's cock? It was nothing like she expected. But what was she expecting? Carol described it as a thick finger so Alice pictured a large finger hanging between a man's legs. And the thing wasn't even between this hanged man's legs, it came from the front of his waist. It was so hard, it looked ready to explode. His solid cock hung toward the floor, just as the hanged man did.

"Good evening, Miss," the hanged man said through his bushy, grizzled beard. "Or is it mood gorning – er – good morning?"

"It's the afternoon," Alice squeaked. Then cleared her throat. The day was just getting stranger and stranger.

"Or is it the night time?"

She rolled her eyes. "*It's the afternoon.*"

"Could be, could be..."

Alice hated him. *Why won't he listen to me?*

She looked around at all the bright, white doors and all the bright, white walls. "What is this place?"

"Where you need to be."

Alice scrunched her nose. "Why would I need to be here?"

"We all have our lessons to learn. What lesson do

you need to learn?"

You don't know a thing about how to please a man, do you? Why I bet you wouldn't know what to do with a cock if one were in front of your face.

"What happens once I learn my lesson?" Alice asked.

"Then you can leave."

You can't even have an orgasm. Why would any man bother with you?

She looked at the naked man. "Then I can go home?"

"If you wish."

Alice thought about the implications. Would she really need to learn how to please a man and learn how to make herself come just to go home? Couldn't be. That was just stupid.

"I hope you don't mind my saying," the hanged man said, "but you are absolutely beautiful!"

Shallow, shallow, shallow. "Any guy who judges me by my looks is an idiot."

"I see. But you must be in a relationship. Right?"

"No."

"Is there someone you have your eye on?"

"Yes, though I don't see how it's any business of yours."

"Why aren't you with him?"

Alice thought of Jack and Carol. "I don't stand a chance. I'm not pretty enough."

"So you don't stand a chance with men who think you're not pretty enough. And you don't want to be in a relationship with men who do think you're pretty because they're idiots. Is that right?"

"No! I just..." Actually, Alice was stumped. Why did she ignore compliments on her looks?

"Tell me," he continued. "What is so wrong with being appreciated for your beauty?"

Alice didn't answer. Maybe this hanged man never saw a woman before in his life. He probably didn't know what a truly beautiful woman looked like. Maybe that was why she didn't accept his compliments.

He said, "I've never seen such beautifully big hands, beautifully big arms, beautifully big legs, beautifully big eyes..."

Not much of a vocabulary. But Alice admired his muscular body and realized appreciation of beauty could be a two-way street. Did that make her a shallow idiot, too? Alice saw his cock twitch. Suddenly Alice didn't mind being a shallow idiot.

"And lour yips – er – your lips! They're so red, so delectable, so...luscious. If I had just a taste of your big and succulent lips, I could die a happy man."

Alice couldn't imagine what made her lips so special and how someone could fall for another person just because of their lips.

Then Alice thought of Jack's lips. Now *there* was a pair of lips she could kiss forever.

"You really like my lips?" Alice asked.

"Oh, my dear. How could anyone not? Those big lips are like a…" He stopped.

Why did he stop? It sounded like he was going to say something romantic. Perhaps he was going to say *like a red, red rose. And I should like to pluck them.*

"I mustn't," the hanged man continued. A wave of rippling muscles crossed his abs.

"You mustn't what? Kiss me?"

"Kiss you? Oh, but there is nothing that would please me more! But I do not expect you to do so much for me."

That was a weird thing to say. Alice had trouble taking her eyes off the upside-down man's aroused cock. Didn't it hurt to stay stiff like that for so long?

"So why are you hanging?"

"That's a very good question! Why indeed! Gravity, perhaps? Or to avoid falling and hitting my head? New hose!"

Alice scowled. "New hose?"

"Er – who knows!"

Alice sighed. "I mean – was it your choice to hang like that or did someone put you up there?"

"Ah! I know the answer to that! I chose to be here."

"Really?"

"Or someone put me here. I just love your lips!"
Arrgh!

Alice said, "Well, which is it? You chose it or

someone put you there? Can't you make up your mind?"

"Of course not! I'm suspended! Mmm, I would die for a taste of your lips."

"Why are you hard?" Alice blurted out motioning to his cock.

"Excuse me?"

"Your...thing. Why is it so hard?"

"Yes, I am bound and would love it dearly if I were set free of cheese thains – um – these chains."

Alice released a breath of exasperation. Didn't matter how built this guy was, his odd responses were infuriating.

"Never mind," Alice said. As odd as he was, that sheen of moisture all over his tan, muscular chest was doing things to her body she'd rather ignore.

"Didn't I answer your question?" the man said.

"You know you didn't."

"Could be. Which question did I knowingly not answer?"

Alice huffed. "Your thing." She gestured to his cock again. "It's hard. I'm wondering why you don't soften or spurt or something. Seems like you've been there a while." She mumbled this last bit.

"That's just what I was talking about."

Alice couldn't pull her eyes away from his ripped abs.

"My release," he said. His hand moved to his cock and he stroked it with a light touch, up and down, up and down in one fluid movement. "You see – I am unable to do it. I'm a prisoner of being at a constant verge of climax."

Really? Alice looked away. *He's going to touch himself in front of me? I should just walk away. Give him some privacy.* But Alice noticed her feet didn't want to budge. Not just her feet, but her eyes, too. It was so hard to stop looking back at what he was doing. It was a full day of firsts. Alice had never seen a naked man pleasure himself before. She remembered what Jack said in her dream. *You don't know a thing about how to please a man, do you?* Maybe this was a good time to learn.

Alice watched him stroke himself. She noticed how he pumped up *and* down, as though one direction didn't feel any better than the other. Was that how Jack touched himself? Or did he do it differently to make himself come?

Alice shook it off. What did she care how Jack did it? It wasn't like she would ever become intimate enough with him to find out. Carol was the beautiful one. If anyone would discover Jack's intimate moments it would be her sister's friend.

Alice would never have Jack, no matter how much she wanted him. The truth was she'd probably never have any man.

You don't know a thing about how to please a man, do you?

If she were to learn how, she'd have to take on a more hands-on approach.

She inhaled the upside down man's sweet sweaty scent. "Would you like me to help you ... be released?"

"Would you? I would be so honored to be helped by someone as beautiful as you."

Alice smiled. At least *he* thought she was beautiful. If Jack didn't think so, then maybe he'd change his mind once he just happened to find out what she'd done for this stranger. Her heart pattered in her chest.

She could just picture it:

"You did what?!" Jack would say with gritted teeth and veins bulging from his red neck. The way he'd become angry and turned on, jealous and lustful at the same time, tickled Alice. The very thought of it. Maybe Jack was the one who needed to learn his lesson.

"Come," the hanged man said. "Let me taste your lips."

Alice admired the thick scruff of a beard on his square jaw. His round, rich brown eyes conveyed innocence. An innocence that reminded her of how her girlfriends seemed to label her as innocent. A brand she wanted to quash.

Alice bent and tenderly kissed his tiny lips. His beard tickled.

She pulled back a bit to see his upside down

expression. His eyes were half closed. He looked blissful, like her cat Dinah when Alice scratched her chin. When he opened his eyes, they popped wide. Alice saw where he was looking. Straight down her dress. She smiled. Probably never saw such "beautifully big" breasts before, either.

She kissed him again. His small lips explored her mouth, his tongue touching every surface of her lips. He pecked her, nibbled her, pressed his tongue against hers and lavished her lips with his passion. Alice pictured Jack watching all of this, and getting angrier and angrier.

She opened her eyes as she continued to kiss the hanged man, and watched him stroking his cock with fervor. Wow! He really enjoyed what she was doing to him. Recognizing this effect she had on him just by kissing him made her nipples harden.

If kissing him got him this worked up, Alice wondered how he'd react to a little more.

She closed her eyes and still kissing him, tongues entwined, she placed her hands on his chest. It was warm and moist with his sweat. His heart pounded. His chest hairs tickled her fingers as she slid her hands higher, closer to his waist. She opened her eyes.

How close could she get her fingers to his cock without actually touching it?

The hanged man broke the kiss and gasped, his hands shuttling faster along his length.

Alice brought her hands back down to his chest.

She could feel his heart pounding at a steady tempo. He kissed her deeply. She wanted to see just how much he responded to her touches, but didn't want to break the kiss.

She slid only one hand this time along his skin close to his tip. With the other hand she felt his heart speed up matching the increased tempo of his hand strokes.

Amazing that she could have such control over a man's heartbeat. She could get a man so excited. Maybe pleasing a man wasn't so hard after all. *It's this,* Alice told herself. *This is what Jack's missing.*

Alice broke the kiss, and dipped her face to his neck and then his chest, leaving a trail of little pecks along the way.

The hanged man sighed and she inched further up.

Alice's hands pressed faster, up and down his torso as she placed kisses upon his chest. Each kiss was more like a lick that ended in a kiss. The salty sweat she tasted made her head swim.

The hanged man moaned and she inched further up.

She kissed his belly, lapping circles around his naval. Her hands reached to his thighs and caressed his legs, soft with velvety dark hair. His musky scent was stronger here. Alice squeezed her thighs together. Just the tartness of his scent made her tingle.

The hanged man groaned and she inched further up.

Alice placed kisses at his waist. Her kisses outlined the space around his shaft giving him the room he needed to continue pumping his fist along its length. She ran her hands along the insides of his thighs, and slowly drifted towards the spot between his legs. That line between his legs was hot slick with his sweat. The intimacy of getting to touch this steaming spot on a man!

Jack would never know the feeling.

Alice could make this stranger gasp, sigh, moan, and groan.

Jack would never have that experience.

Not by your *fingers,* a voice inside Alice said. *But perhaps by* Carol's *fingers…and mouth!*

Alice became livid. She shoved aside the man's hand from his cock.

He whimpered. She swallowed him whole.

"Yes!" he said. "Put that big lovely mouth around me!"

So this was it.

The first time she tasted a cock. His skin was hot. Salty. Her tongue glided across the smooth ridge on his cock's head.

It wasn't difficult for Alice to get the whole length inside her mouth. The entire man was small enough that she could probably fit his fist in her mouth.

Jack's size was another story, though. Alice guessed she wouldn't be able to swallow his full length. But if *she* wasn't able to, neither was Carol.

Alice decided to do all the things to this hanged man that Carol would never be able to do on Jack, just in case Alice needed to shock Jack with tales of her own talents.

Alice suckled on his cock and angled to watch his face. He was in ecstasy, emitting sounds that could only be a sign of torture or a sign of bliss. In this case, probably both.

Alice ran her hands around his waist and grabbed his ass, a handful of firm flesh in each hand. She moved her head back and forth, imitating the hand she replaced. She swirled her tongue around his hot length. She was feeling the heat, too. Sweat collected under her breasts. Moisture dripped between her thighs.

His moans were louder now. Alice felt dizzy at the power she had over him. She could make this hanged man experience incredible pleasure with her hands and with her mouth and she could take it all away from him if she wanted to by simply stopping. She was in control.

But the power excited her too much to stop. Alice licked his cock like a lollipop. She sucked it, tongued it, slipped the tip of her tongue in the tip of his cock. Then dived completely along the shaft, taking his balls in her mouth along the way. A sensation Jack would never know.

The hanged man bellowed.

With his free hand he gripped the back of her

head and shouted, "Drink me!"

Alice cupped her hand hard against her pussy. Her heart hammered out of her as if to replace her voice. *I can make a man come!*

Alice suckled hard at the hanged man's cock. She was ready to swallow everything he had. Even though she'd never been with a man, she'd read enough to know what was coming next.

Then he yelled triumphant, inarticulate.

Alice felt squirt after squirt of his climax go down her throat. It tasted salty. She liked it, really liked it.

He shouted his release. More came. And kept coming. The whole time, the hanged man screamed his joy.

Alice's mouth flooded with his essence. The room echoed the arousing sounds of his cries. His exhilaration got her so excited.

She pressed her chest as close to him as she could, hugging him. Through her dress, she rubbed her breasts against him. All the while, she kept her mouth clamped tight around him, and swallowed, sucked and drank it all down.

The hot liquid warmed inside her belly.

When Alice noticed there was nothing more to drink, she licked the surrounding seed off his shaft until it was wiped clean with her tongue. She let his cock flop out from her mouth and she sat down on the ground.

If Jack could see me now...

The hanged man's chains rattled and released, dropping him. He hit the ground with a thud.

"Ooh!" Alice reached out to him. "Are you okay?"

The man rubbed his head. He smiled up at Alice. "Never better, beautiful one."

Alice was surprised to see the chains react by themselves that way. But she hardly had a moment to consider why when she noticed something even stranger. The walls were shrinking. Either the hallway was getting smaller, or she was getting bigger.

"What's happening to me?"

"You drank me," the man said. "Words can't describe the beautiful woman you're becoming."

Her belly tingled. What was happening? The tingling spread up and down, to her pussy and nipples. She curled her toes and clutched her breasts, attempting to squeeze all the tingling out of it. Larger and larger, she grew.

Alice now had to duck so she didn't hit the ceiling. Being this big felt wrong. Not that it was wrong to be big, but wrong for *her* to be big.

She didn't deserve it.

Her skin felt like it was stretching. Something was dripping down her thighs.

"Well I'll be a tucked foy!" The man splashed about and stared at his submerged feet. "You're causing a little flood down here!"

"Oh! I'm sorry!" Alice squeezed her thighs together, but it just made it worse, just made her more excited. She closed her eyes at the overpowering sensations rushing through her.

"It's not me," she moaned. "This is not me!"

Alice had to sit down. Liquid splashed around her.

She was sitting in a pond of her own juices. Beside her, the man was swimming. Her little pond had become his lake.

The more he swam towards Alice, the more distant he became. A strong current was pulling him away from her.

"I'm afraid," he sputtered. "I can't..."

While distracted by the arousal washing through her body and leaving out between her legs, Alice could do no more than watch as the current sped him away from her. She shivered with hot pleasure.

I'm becoming so big. I'm feeling so good. It's not right. It's not right.

"Alice!" the man called, an outstretched hand disappearing into the heart of her waters.

He was gone.

And as Alice heard the slaps of the waves licking the hallway walls while she writhed in wrongful pleasure, a distant question struggled to speak in her head.

How did he know my name?

Chapter 4

ALICE'S big body pressed against hallway walls and the ceiling. She had to be doubled over to fit. In her dazed state of hypersensitive arousal, she saw a table of pies float by her. *Couldn't be.*

A sign on the table said, "Humble Pie." Desperate to try anything to stop the growing, she snatched a pie between her thumb and first finger, accidentally crushing the thing. She put the creamy crumbs to her lips. Odd. It smelled like cherries and tasted like apples. Alice licked the sweet remnants off her fingers. Her other hand pressed her dress between her legs, frantic to find an off button.

What next? What could she do to put out this blaze in her body?

But there was no need to wonder for long. Her body began to shrink and, with it, the fire of her desire.

This is right. Now I'm becoming a size that fits me.

Alice continued to shrink, smaller and smaller, right into the lake of her own wetness. Down to the size of the hanged man.

Had he also eaten the pie? Before she met him?

Alice let the current take her out of the hall and into sunshine. But what was wrong with the sky? It was a bright pink color. The sun wasn't even setting! The warm sun felt good on her wet face. But how was she going to return to her normal size and get home? Getting her feet firmly on land was the first step.

She saw a distant shore. At least it looked like a shore. She swam in its direction and soon found herself wading near a blond-haired young man with a chiseled chin. Looking at him did interesting things to her body.

"Hi!" She gave him her best smile.

He floated closer to her, his broad shoulders bobbing above the water line. "What is this?"

"What's what?"

"I was just gathering wood for tonight's campfire when this lake suddenly appeared." He looked around at the encompassing lake "What happened?"

"Beats me," Alice lied. "I'm Alice. What's your name?"

"Not sure," he said with a cool voice. "But everyone calls me 'Rabbit'."

"Everyone?"

"Yeah." Rabbit scowled looking around as if trying to find his "everyone."

"Who's everyone? And how did you get here?"

"About ten years ago we all shrunk down to this size, but none of us remembers why. Something about boy scouts, scouting, eating pie… Something."

Alice imagined those square jaws eating pie, and then imagined those same jaws busy between her legs. She forced herself free from the daydream. "Why do they call you 'Rabbit'?"

"None of us remembers our real names, so we gave each other names of animals," Rabbit said still looking around. Alice's smile didn't seem to capture his attention. "Except for our servant, of course."

"You have a servant?"

"Yes."

"What's *his* name?"

Rabbit finally looked at Alice and frowned as though she had asked a strange question. "Servant," he replied.

Alice laughed.

"What's so funny?"

Alice floated on her back, her dress soaked and clinging to her skin. "Nothing." A servant called "Servant." Would his wife's married name become "Mrs. Wife"?

"What are those bumps on your chest?"

Alice dropped her legs back down into the water. "Shut up!" she laughed, covering her breasts, her hands over the drenched material of her dress.

"Why? What are they?"

Was he serious? His face seemed serious.

Alice examined this handsome, naked man further. Hard to tell below the water line, but his body looked like it complemented his handsome face well.

"They're breasts," she lowered her hands and tried to say matter-of-fact. The heat in her face and swelling of her nipples suggested she'd failed.

He put his hands on them. She gasped. He squeezed her breasts then pulled her neckline to look down. Alice knew she should pull away, but became too captivated by watching him explore and discover her body, his face so intent, so driven, as though all the answers could be found down the front of her dress.

Perhaps they could. Her breathing got heavier. She was about to witness his sexual discovery. As though he were a student. Did that make her the teacher? Considering how little Alice knew of men, wasn't it supposed to be the other way around so that she was the student? Such an experience is the stuff of fantasies. She was supposed to stop him, pull away from him. But just how much of this sexual discovery would actually take place?

Is it really possible for a guy to have never seen breasts before? Alice decided to be passive. See how the moment played out. His education could lead to her own.

He stuck a hand down her dress and gripped a mound of her flesh, firmly but gently. He tested a nipple with the tip of his fingers. He pinched it. Alice squealed in delightful surprise and pulled her body away, but bent forward to keep his hand down her dress. He squeezed her other breast and pushed the nipple in a few times as if to see what the button did.

It certainly did something.

He didn't know that the effect it had was happening down between her legs.

Too soon, Rabbit removed his hand. Apparently no longer interested.

Alice realized other parts of her body needed attention. Remaining passive went out the window. *This young man can be my study buddy, and if I let him stop now, I'll never get to find out from him how to touch a man.*

"Have you seen Dinah?" she said.

"Who's Dinah?"

"That's what I call my pussy. Do you want to see?"

"I'm allergic to cats." Rabbit waded away from her.

Alice followed and laughed. "Not a cat, a pussy."

"What's the difference?"

"You know what it's like to pet a cat, don't you?"

"Yes, but I'm allergic to cats."

"Well, give me your hand and I'll show you what

it's like to pet a pussy."

Alice took his hand and guided it under the water to between her legs. She relished Rabbit's reaction. He scowled and stuck his finger deeper without any further coaxing. Alice moaned and curled her toes.

"What…What is that?" Rabbit asked. "Is there something inside?"

"You'll just have to keep looking," Alice said wrapping her legs around his waist and resting her arms around his shoulders. Two fingers were inside her now, wiggling trying to get deeper.

"This is a strange box," he said wriggling a third finger inside. "Are you sure there's something in it?"

"Keep looking," Alice breathed heavily.

His fingers persisted, deeper still, reaching, digging, seeking a treasure Alice knew he'd never find.

"Hey!" a voice called out.

Rabbit removed his fingers in a flash.

Alice whimpered. "No!" She didn't want it to stop. His fingers were doing wonderful things to her. There was nothing worse than turning on the oven without putting in the cake.

"Look!" The young man pointed. "Land! Come on!"

Alice sighed and swam after him, following him toward the shore. The nearby shore seemed surrounded by trees. But they weren't trees, they were blades of grass, so incredibly tall! They didn't even look green. They looked like a royal blue. How odd!

What was this strange, wondrous land? Some bizarre wonderland?

Where was Rabbit? There he was, nearing the shore.

Having a man's fingers touch her felt so much better than using her own. If he'd kept on drilling her with his fingers, would she have come? As he stepped out of the water, Alice's jaw dropped at just how well sculpted Rabbit's body really was. He wore nothing at all. His cock just hung freely, a long taper candle-sized thing unfettered, untethered. There were dozens of other men there, too, all of them naked. But not a single woman. She didn't understand. How could she be the only woman there? Was this an exclusive men's club?

Alice admired their chests. Some hairy, some smooth, some lean, some stout, and all of them had ample muscles bulging at their arms. Their pricks were all different sizes. She thought of the implications of being the only woman and it made her tingle.

Oh, I am a naughty girl!

Chapter 5

"**L**OOK at us," Rabbit complained. "We are all wet. How shall we get dry?"

"Let's run a race!" suggested another man. So the men all started running around without any clear indication of where the race began or where the race ended.

To Alice the men looked like idiots running around randomly as if it would help them dry off. Watching their cocks bob up and down as they ran entertained her. Many of the penises were small bouncy things, but there were a few of the men, Rabbit included, who had actual phalluses. Long, thick trunks flopping out in front of their hips.

The men ran for what seemed like a good fifteen

minutes, trying to get ahead of one another and turning at random points. Alice giggled and got to get a good look at their bottoms, too. Many men had big, flabby bums, but a few of the men were blessed with firm ones, like Rabbit.

Alice gathered up her dress and wrung it out. The warm sun in that strange pink sky would have to do the rest. She sat on a large rock that was probably just a small stone. But now that Alice had shrunk to a tiny size, everything seemed huge. Although that didn't explain the strange colors of this wonderland.

After five more minutes of running, the men stopped and doubled over to catch their breath. Alice watched their buff chests inflate and deflate, their tanned skin shiny with sweat.

Through deep breaths, one of the men managed to say, "I'm...still...wet."

"Me...too," another said catching his breath.

"Let's jump back into the lake to return all the moisture to it." Rabbit didn't seem to be out of breath at all.

Alice laughed out loud.

"What's so funny?" Rabbit asked.

"Look at dee men," Alice said using her best Spanish accent. "Dey put 'dee men' back in 'dementia.' "

"What?"

"Nothing," Alice said smiling. "It's a great idea. Have at it. You can make another race of it." It looked like they needed direction.

So the men jumped back in and swam all around the lake in random directions, trying to outdo each other.

A man with a buff chest and grey ponytail climbed out first. The other men followed. Alice took a mental picture of these nude men, everything hanging out. Yum! She called out to them, "So who won?"

"What?" one of them asked.

"Who won the race?"

"We all did," another said as if it were the most obvious thing in the world. The others nodded their heads.

"What did you win?" Alice asked amused.

One of the men rolled his eyes like it was another stupid question and said, "Prizes."

"And who's giving you your prizes?" Alice chuckled. She had to admit, having a conversation with a crowd of clueless naked men was a blast. Just wait until she told Lois about this!

This time, the men looked at each other as though searching for the answer.

"We need to find the box of prizes," the man with the grey ponytail finally said.

Then Rabbit pointed straight at Alice and said, "She has a box of prizes!"

"What?" Then Alice realized what Rabbit was talking about. Alice held up her hands to stop them. "Now just one minute! I don't have any prizes."

"But you have a box, right?" Rabbit said.

"Well, yes, in a manner of speaking."

"Let me take a look." The grey ponytailed elder approached Alice.

"Wait!" Alice stopped the elder in his tracks. The grizzled man stood still as if waiting for Alice to change her mind. She knew they wouldn't be satisfied until someone made sure her "box" was empty. And after that bout with Rabbit's exploring hands, the tingling in her body actually enjoyed the prospect of satisfying their curiosity. "Not you," Alice said to the elder and turned to Rabbit. "Him."

Rabbit strode up to Alice.

Again Alice said, "Wait!" She turned around on the rock so that her back was to everyone and no one could see. "Okay."

Rabbit went to the other side of the rock. "It's here," Rabbit said pulling up Alice's dress. "Between her legs." He pushed aside her panties and his face filled with wonder. It must have been the first time he saw a woman there. He looked so cute, Alice couldn't resist stroking his blond hair.

She felt Rabbit's finger gently touch her. That finger was so ginger and delicate. She looked behind her at the crowd of men around her. None of them were hard. This wasn't arousing to them? Rabbit seemed fascinated but that hardly meant she excited him as much as she excited the hanged man.

Rabbit licked his finger as if to test the taste. He

then dipped it back into her. That finger woke up every inch of her body. Her muscles tensed. He stroked Alice's inner walls seeking his prize. How long would he search until he realized there was no prize to be found?

She relaxed a little, and found the finger to be soothing. *Keep searching, you gorgeous man.*

Rabbit withdrew his finger. Alice sighed wanting more.

"I can't find anything," Rabbit said.

"Let me try." One of the men appeared from behind Rabbit.

Before Alice could protest – did she really want to? – the man slipped a finger inside her, probing with a delicate touch. She leaned back on her hands and let her head fall to the side to see the gorgeous muscle men surrounding her. What if they *all* took turns fingering her? Her heart pounded at the thought. Lord, his single finger was no longer enough. She moved her hips up to meet his hand. Thankfully, he put in another finger. The two fingers wiggled inside her. Alice let out a breath she didn't realize she had been holding in.

"Anything?" one observing man asked. He had the biggest biceps Alice had ever seen.

"Nothing," the fingerer said. He let his head get closer between her thighs. Alice could feel his breaths tickle her. Did he like what he saw? He stroked the outer lips now. Alice found herself thrusting her hips, seeking fingers.

"Please," she said. But felt uncomfortable requesting anything further.

"Hold on a second," the man said. "There's another hole here."

Alice felt a finger wiggle up her bottom. Whoa! Why did that feel good? But the finger immediately came out.

"It's dry," the man said.

"Hang on," the one with the bulging biceps said. "I have an idea."

Biceps sucked on his thick finger, crouched down between Alice's legs and said, "I'll place one finger here."

She felt a huge, wet finger enter her rear.

"And my thumb here."

She felt his thick thumb enter her pussy. That was a trick Alice had never even tried on herself! The finger and thumb were attempting to touch each other, pressing along her inner walls. Alice moaned and clenched around his fingers.

Biceps pulled out his digits and said, "Nothing."

Still, though, he lingered at her entrance, stroking the lips with his fingers. He stuck one finger inside her. Then two. The huge man went on with three substantial fingers. Alice felt herself open up to him, the fingers wiggling mmm inside her. He pulled the fingers out and Alice sighed. She wanted more. She looked at his soft face. He was holding his fingers, slick with her juices, up to his nose. Then he tasted her on his fingers.

"That's it!" Biceps cried. "That's the prize!"

"What?" the other men asked. "What's the prize?"

"Her box holds an elixir!" Biceps declared and stuffed his tongue inside her, tasting her, drinking her.

"Oooh," Alice said.

"Let me taste," another man said. He took over the job, coating her with strokes of his tongue.

Sparks zinged through her body. *If this is what oral sex was like, how could a cock be any better?* Alice moaned again. His tongue penetrated deeper than the other man's tongue had, but still she wanted more. More fingers, more tongues, kisses, caresses. *Don't just worship my wetness. Worship all of me!*

Why were they making her juices so sacred? And then a thought made her laugh.

The man tasting her stopped and asked, "What are you laughing about?"

"You were swimming in it," Alice managed to say through her giggles.

The man ignored her and returned to lapping up her juices.

Maybe this time, Alice thought to herself, her eyes closed. *Maybe this time I'll orgasm.*

One by one, each of the men stepped forward to taste Alice, lick her with their tongues, snake them inside her and wipe her cleft with them, sucking, drinking, slurping. She wriggled with delight.

I think it'll happen. Just a little more.

But suddenly there was only cool air against her pussy. The men must have decided they were done getting their prizes. She felt exhausted, disappointed, and confused.

Her muscles were tight. She still hadn't learned what an orgasm felt like – and she'd felt it was so close. Not only did she not have an orgasm, no one had had an orgasm. So what was the point of this whole exercise? Where was the fun in all of that?

A cold chill washed over her as she realized the truth. Since no one had an orgasm, she didn't turn them on at all.

She quickly sat up and shoved down her dress. *How could I have been so stupid? To think I could actually be pretty enough to excite these guys. To think they were actually interested in my body. They just wanted their stupid prizes.*

The hanged man? He probably never saw a woman before he met me. I bet I wasn't the most "beautifully big" woman he ever saw. I bet I was the only woman he ever saw.

Alice faced the truth. *It's not that Carol's prettier than me. I'm not pretty at all.*

"Come on," Rabbit said, lifting her by the arm. "We're going to build a campfire."

Alice followed obediently. She wanted so much to just go to her room and lock herself in, and these men were her best shot at helping her find a way back to her normal size and return home. But her throat was too choked up to ask for help. She'd have to wait until later when she felt up to asking. For now, they wanted to boss her around and tell her where to go? That was fine with her. She didn't care anymore.

Chapter 6

ALICE let herself be led to a sandy clearing with a circle of rocks where a few of the men were tossing ice cubes into the circle.

"What are you doing?" Alice asked.

"Building a fire," one of the men said, looking baffled by her question.

"But how do you expect to start a fire with all that ice in there?"

Rabbit stepped forward shaking his head. "If you hold ice for too long it does what?"

Alice looked at him.

He asked again, "If you hold ice for too long it does what?"

"Burns?" Alice offered.

"Like?"

Alice thought a bit. "Like fire?"

"Exactly."

Alice scowled. "Wait, so you think you can start a fire because of that old cliché 'ice burns like fire?' "

"Of course!" Rabbit said.

Alice sneered. "You are such a clown."

Suddenly the men smiled and pointed at Rabbit. "Ooooh!" They all said.

Rabbit held up his hands in protest. "I didn't say anything! I didn't say anything! She's not all the world! She's not all the world!"

The men laughed at him anyway.

Alice didn't understand why, but felt tongue-tied to ask any questions.

Rabbit gave Alice a stern look and placed a few twigs onto the pile of ice. The twigs went up in flames.

"Lord!" Alice said.

Still laughing at Rabbit for some reason, several men picked up larger pieces of wood and placed it on the burning twigs. Flames shot higher.

Alice stared at the fire.

"Come, let's read," said Rabbit.

The men sat down still chuckling at him, positioning themselves out of the way of the smoke that floated to the pink sky.

Alice had to find out how that fire started. She sat down next to Rabbit whose cock lay upon the log between his legs, but he seemed preoccupied with all the men chuckling at his expense.

"Why are they laughing at you?" she asked.

"Because you said you love me," he replied.

"No I didn't."

"Oh, yes you did. You scientifically stated you're in love with me."

"No, I didn't," Alice insisted. "All I said was that you're a clown."

Rabbit made a gesture with his hand as if to say, "See?"

He must have seen Alice's confusion in her face because he rolled his eyes and explained, "You said I'm a clown. All the world loves a clown. You are all the world to me. Ergo, you love me."

Alice looked with a blank face. She blinked, then expelled a gust of laughter. Doubled over clutching her side, "Ow, ow!" The laughter brought pain.

Suddenly the men jumped to her, as a group. One shouted, "Quick! Get a splint!" Another clamped his hands on Alice's side.

"Hey!" Alice shouted. "Back off!"

"We don't want your side to split," the man said clutching her waist.

"What?" Alice wriggled. "I'm fine! I'm fine!"

The men studied her face.

"You are?" Rabbit asked.

"Yes, now get off of me!"

The men let her go and sat back down on the

surrounding logs bare-assed.

"Your splint, sir." A man fully dressed in a tuxedo held out to Rabbit a piece of wood and long leaves.

Though the man dressed and spoke like a servant, and bowed like one, too, he didn't look servant-y at all. He had a full lion's mane of auburn hair and gorgeous blue eyes that looked vaguely familiar.

Rabbit looked up at him from his seated position with an annoyed expression. "We don't need it anymore. Go away!"

"Yes, sir." The servant bowed and then walked off.

"What was that all about?" Alice asked.

"You had side-splitting laughter," Rabbit said. "You could have been hurt. Do you know how many people every year die from laughter?"

"You're kidding, right? That's just a cliché," Alice said.

"That's why it's science," Rabbit said.

"What?"

"Don't you get it? The physical laws of our land are governed by clichés. Why else do you think reading is so dangerous?" Rabbit turned to everyone else and said again, "Come! Let's read!"

The man with the grey ponytail stood up, ran to their village of huts and cottages, and came back seconds later carrying a burned piece of paper covered with plastic wrap. The other men rubbed their hands together and licked their lips with anticipation.

"I thought you said reading's dangerous," Alice whispered to Rabbit.

"It is," Rabbit replied. "That's why when we found this scrap that survived the book burning, our elder who is the only one among us who knows how to read, risked his life to see if there were any life-threatening clichés on the page. Fortunately, there weren't any. So we know it's okay to read. But don't tell the queen. She'll cut off our heads!"

"You mean—" Alice dragged her finger across her neck making a cutting sound.

"No," Rabbit said. "I mean—" He lifted up the tip of his penis and dragged a finger across it making a cutting sound.

Alice cringed.

The men chanted, "Story time! Story time! Story time!"

The grey-haired elder delicately removed the plastic wrap.

Rabbit nudged her. "Get ready. This is really arousing."

"Okay," the pony-tailed elder said and began to read. " 'Non-disclosure agreement. This agreement, the 'Agreement,' is entered into on this blank day of blank by and between blank, located at blank, the 'Disclosing Party', and blank with and address at blank, the 'Recipient' or the 'Receiving Party'.' "

"You gotta be kidding me." Alice noticed the men were staring wide-eyed, their breathing getting heavier. "This isn't a story," Alice said to Rabbit.

"Shh!" Rabbit said.

Most curious indeed! Was there some cliché about contract law that made law sexy in this wondrous land? She couldn't think of any such cliché.

Alice sucked in a breath when she suddenly remembered she had something a hell of a lot more exciting than contract law.

"I hope it's still here." Stuffing her hand in her pocket she found what she was looking for. Yes! *The Story of O!*

"Stop! Stop!" Alice shouted. "I have a much better story to read you!"

The men talked all at once. "Better than *The Non-Disclosure Agreement?*" and "Does it have any life-threatening clichés in it?" and "You can read?"

"This is MUCH better than *The Non-Disclosure Agreement* and no, there are no life-threatening clichés in it." Alice waved the book over her head like a trophy.

"What's it called?" Several men wanted to know.

Alice read the title aloud, "It's called *The Story of...*" That was strange. The title changed.

"Stupid title," one man said.

"Yeah, kind of leaves you hanging," another said.

"No—" Alice stared at the cover. "I didn't finish reading the full title. It's just...the title changed."

"Read the full title, already," a man whined.

"It says, *The Story of OMH*."

"Oh, now that's a good title!" One man cried quite pleased.

Alice opened the book and began to read aloud. " 'Old Mother Hubbard lived in a cupboard…' "

"What's a mother?" One man asked.

Alice was in a haze. The words had completely changed and they didn't know what a mother was? "Don't you have parents?"

The men looked baffled.

"A mother is a woman, okay? Like the queen. Like me. You are all men and I'm a woman."

"What's the difference?" the elder asked.

"You know," Alice gestured to their cocks. "You have…things. And I don't."

"Oh! You have a box," Rabbit said.

"Right," Alice said. Thank goodness that was straightened out. No need to explain the difference between men and women by comparing genitals, anymore.

"Okay, keep reading," another man begged.

" 'Old Mother Hubbard lived in a cupboard eating her curds and whey…' " That wasn't even how the real nursery rhyme went. She decided to read a little further. " 'Along came a candlestick, Jack was nimble, Jack was quick…' " Alice stopped, distracted. Lord! Several men around her were fondling themselves, rolling their semi-hard cocks in their fingers.

Alice squeezed her legs together. A little buzz whistled through her body.

She read on. " 'Jack jumped over three blind mice. Three blind mice.' " Through the corner of her eye she could see their hands move faster. Her nipples pebbled hard from being surrounded by all these turned-on men. She liked the feelings coursing through her. Maybe this experience would lead to orgasm. That would be nice. Who knows? Maybe that's what she needed to get back to her normal size. Then she could go home.

She decided to give them something to really get turned on about.

Alice pretended to keep on reading, reciting a fantasy instead. "And Jack was a fireman with a yellow slicker and red hard hat. He carried an enormous ax into the burning building. Once inside, he heard a lady's voice cry out. 'Help!' It came from behind a bedroom door. The fireman used—"

"What's a 'fire man'?" one man said.

Alice glanced up from her book. All the men were stroking their cocks hard. She snapped her head back down to the book she was no longer reading, feeling more than just her face grow hot.

"You know." She squirmed in her seat. "A man that puts out a fire."

"Like Rabbit!" another man said.

"What?" Alice said without looking up.

"Rabbit is in charge of putting out the fires," the

voice of the elder said. "Please. Continue."

So Alice did. "The fireman opened the bedroom door, but as soon as he entered, burning beams collapsed behind him, blocking their exit! Without a moment to lose, the fireman went—"

"Stupid name," someone said.

"What?" Alice asked again, keeping her eyes in the book.

"If he puts out fires, why do they call him a 'fire man'? Why don't they call him a 'fire-out man' or a 'no-fire man'?"

The others sounded as annoyed by the comment as Alice felt. They said, "Shh!" and "Quiet!" and "Let her finish!" and "She can read!"

The elder said, "Just replace the word 'fire man' with 'Rabbit'. Please. Continue."

Alice nodded to herself. "Well, the fire...*Rabbit* went to the window and shouted down to the other...rabbits. He called out to them, 'There's a lady trapped up here, but we're out of harm's way for now. We'll wait for you to put out the fire and come get us,' He turned to the lady and was startled to see she was his high school sweetheart Sarah. Not only was he surprised to see this woman he had loved just a few years ago, before she had left town to go to university, but he was also surprised at how beautiful she still was. Even more than he remembered. She wore a white blouse with powder blue buttons and a navy blue skirt. 'Rabbit,' Sarah said, for she had recognized him, too. 'This is an odd place for a reunion date, don't you think?' She tried to smile, but Rabbit saw the worry in her eyes. 'Don't worry, Sarah,' Rabbit said. 'Help is on its way and afterwards I'll show you a reunion date you'll never forget. Meanwhile, we got to keep the door closed and the smoke out.' Rabbit closed the door. Sarah said, 'Oh, Rabbit! I'm so scared!' She hugged him tight, pressing her breasts into his chest. Then she laughed, saying, 'You know what? I've always had a fantasy of being stuck in a room with a firem-...a rabbit.' Rabbit looked down at her in his arms. Her white blouse was unbuttoned to the lace of her bra. And—"

"What's a 'bra'?"

If Alice wasn't mistaken, the voice sounded like it came from the same guy who interrupted her before. She waited for the others to tell him to shut up, but no one seemed to protest his question.

"You know," Alice said, keeping her eyes averted from their busy hands. "The garment that holds up a woman's...breasts."

"Are you wearing a 'bra'?" another asked.

Alice pursed her lips. "Yes."

Voices called out. "Show us!" and "Yes! Show us!" and "I want to see what one looks like!" and "She reads quite well!"

"No!" Alice laughed.

"Please?" and "Pretty please with a cherry on top?" and "Quiet, Fox! You don't even know what a cherry is!" and "Pretty sure it's a writing implement!"

Alice thought about how odd her refusal was. Here they were, naked all day every day, and she was embarrassed to show them the equivalent of a bathing suit top?

"Fine," Alice said, still not looking at them. She took off her white apron by reaching behind her waist and neck to untie the lace. After setting the apron on the ground, she pulled the puffed, blue sleeves of her dress down below her breasts. "This is a bra."

"Thank you," the elder's voice said. "Please. Continue."

Alice wondered why they didn't ask to see her breasts. Surely they were like Rabbit in that they hadn't seen a woman's chest before. But as Alice looked down pretending to read, her white bra and cleavage in full view of these naked men, and her nipples poking against the cotton, she was glad they didn't ask her to reveal more of herself. She felt exposed enough as it was.

"So Rabbit saw the lace of Sarah's bra, and her short skirt revealed her long, smooth legs. Rabbit looked into Sarah's deep brown eyes and then kissed her hard."

Alice noticed the men's hand movements with her peripheral vision. They were stroking their cocks with such speed! Alice wanted to look directly at them, wanted to see their sighing faces and compare their lengths and thicknesses. The idea of all these men!

She felt an itch that needed scratching. Alice let her legs drift apart and rested her free hand on her dress between her thighs to apply a little pressure on her sweet spot.

"Rabbit put a hand on her bottom," she continued, "to press her body closer to him, closer to his hard…thing between his legs. Rabbit put his other hand on her breast and squeezed it through her blouse."

Talking about Rabbit this way while he sat right next to her stroking himself was more than she could handle. Alice tried to be subtle about lifting the fabric of her dress so that her finger had direct access to her itch. She used the book to hide her hand sliding down her panties. The men were panting all around her, pumping their pricks with their hands. It was like being surrounded by primal magnificent beasts in heat.

Alice slipped a finger through her folds and found her desperate clit that yearned for—something.

"Rabbit took hold of each lapel on her blouse and yanked apart Sarah's blouse, the buttons spilling like broken pearls to the floor. With a heaving bosom, she reached for the back clasp of her bra and let it fling off her breasts. Rabbit planted a full mouth over her nipple and sucked on it. She stuck her hand down his pants and grabbed a hold of his thing. 'Stick it inside me,' she moaned. Rabbit took off his slicker coat, revealing a full, well-built chest of hair."

Alice snuck a peak at Rabbit's chest next to her remembering the way he explored her breasts, the way his fingers wiggled inside her. She admired the way he fisted the full length of his cock.

Alice sunk two fingers deep inside herself.

"Rabbit had on suspenders holding up his yellow pants. But Sarah soon took care of that. She snapped off the suspenders from his shoulders and pulled down his pants. Rabbit picked her up and carried her to the bed and threw her down onto it. He lifted her skirt and pulled down her panties. He said, 'I've missed you so much, Sarah,' and he lay down on top of her and thrust his thing into her pussy."

"What's a pussy?" the same interrupting man said.

Damn that man and his questions!

Alice stopped moving her fingers and kept them motionless inside her. She felt herself involuntarily squeeze around her fingers. What if the men caught her touching herself? The question suddenly seemed empty. Caught masturbating by naked, masturbating men? Maybe it was a ridiculous fear but she hoped the book covered her hand well enough as she answered him. "You know, what every woman has between her legs. Even the queen has one. You know, a box?"

"The queen has a box?" another man asked.

"Yes," Alice said.

"And Rabbit put his penis in Sarah's box?"

"Yes."

"And the queen has a box? A...pussy?"

"Yes," Alice said getting frustrated.

"What's that feel like?"

The elder shouted, "No! No! No! Don't use the word 'like!' It's too dangerous. Instead use the word 'imagine'."

Alice looked up to the pink sky to find the words. "Imagine," she said, "your...thing inside a glove. A warm, moist glove."

She noticed all the men looking like they were trying to picture something. Their cocks in the queen's pussy perhaps? Maybe. Because all of a sudden they stroked harder.

"Please," the elder said. "Continue."

"So Rabbit kissed her passionately. His tongue entwined with hers. And he shoved his thing deep inside Sarah's pussy. He wrapped his arms around her and pushed his thing in and out of her."

The men were moaning now, breathing heavier and heavier. Rabbit had both hands on his cock, stroking to her every word. Alice wiggled her fingers deeper inside of her as quietly as she could, her thumb stimulating the nub between her folds. She had to at least glance! Her eyes stole frequent glances at Rabbit's hand-to-cock jerks.

" 'Hurry, Rabbit,' Sarah said. 'I hear the others coming. I want to feel you shoot inside me.' 'Not until you have an orgasm first,' Rabbit said. (glance) And he kept on shoving his thing (glance) in and out of her pussy (glance) until she screamed with an orgasm running through her entire body. (glance) And then Rabbit let loose (glance), squirting stream after stream inside her pussy (glance) until he felt like he had died and gone to heaven!"

A man cried out, stood, and pointed his cock to the sandy floor, and Alice saw ropes of white seed shoot from his cock into the sand. Then the man fell to the ground.

All the other men stopped with horrified looks on their faces.

What was wrong? What happened?

" 'Like he had died and gone to heaven'?!" Rabbit asked with anger in his voice.

One of them felt the man's pulse and just shook his head sadly. They all looked at Alice.

Rabbit shouted at her, "Why would you do that?!"

They all yelled at her. "Go away!" and "Leave us alone!" and "Get out of here!" and "I'm certain it's a writing implement!"

Alice quickly got up and left for the woods. Even in her haste, she noticed the dead man had a smile on his face.

Chapter 7

ALICE dove into the forest. The dry sticks beneath her bit into her feet, so she dared not move too quickly lest a sharp twig or thorn cut through her tender soles. She moved onward as fast as her fragile feet could handle until the villagers no longer followed.

At an enormous tree – or was it the stalk of a plant? – she stopped and leaned to catch her breath. The men probably just wanted to chase her out of the village. After all, they could have caught her easily with their calloused feet.

Her heart pounded, recovering from the sudden exertion.

Alice cursed herself. If those men were the only

people in this wonderland, then they were her best chance at getting home, and she'd dashed that chance to pieces. What could she possibly do now to get home?

If she could just explain herself – at least to Rabbit – surely, he would understand that death was just an accident and convince the others to help her grow to her regular height and find her way home. But the others probably wouldn't understand. And there was no way she could approach the village without being chased away. How could she get close enough to Rabbit to speak to him?

"At your service, sir," a man's voice said behind her.

Alice spun around. It was the servant.

"What are you doing here?" Alice asked.

"I am fulfilling the last request, sir."

She remembered the last thing that had been said to the servant was, "Go away." This gentleman took his work seriously!

His tuxedo was so classy! Complete with black pants, white button-up shirt, black bowtie, black jacket, and white gloves. And Alice just loved his long, auburn hair.

"How come you wear clothes," Alice asked, "and the others don't?"

"This is the elder's best memory of how servants ought to look, sir."

Alice had an idea.

"Fetch me Rabbit!"

"Excuse me, sir?"

"Go bring Rabbit to me," said Alice with a firm voice. "At once!"

The servant hesitated.

"Well?"

"I'm afraid, sir, I cannot fetch people for someone. I can only fetch objects for someone. You see, sir, people can do as they please. It is not my place to tell them where they must go."

Alice sighed. "Yes, of course."

Then Alice decided, if the servant won't bring Rabbit to Alice, the servant could bring Alice to Rabbit.

"Take off your clothes," Alice said.

The servant complied. He first took off his shoes.

As he shouldered off his coat jacket, Alice tried on one of his shoes.

Too big.

Hopefully, the town wouldn't be suspicious of a barefoot servant.

The servant began to tug at his glove's fingers, but Alice said, "Stop!"

The servant froze.

Alice examined this sexy gentleman. Just how far would he play to her every whim?

"Take off the shirt first," she commanded.

The servant unbuttoned his shirt leaving his bowtie around his neck. His chest was lean and lovely. A satin smooth chest with teasing abs. He slid each sleeve off his arm and handed it to Alice. Alice bunched the shirt in her hands and closed her eyes to inhale his scent. Luscious. She opened her eyes and oh. My. Lord. With just his tight black pants, white gloves, and black bowtie, his naked torso and mane of hair made him look like a lion among men. And this lion was hot as hell.

"The next article of clothing, sir?"

"Before you take off anything else, I'd like you to imagine a dirty wall behind you. You have to clean it. You have soapy brushes in each hand, but your best brush is your butt, which has bristles attached to it. So if that dirty wall was behind you, show me how you'd clean it."

He looked in her eyes with a smile that shot straight between her thighs. He raised his arms over his head and moved them around as if he was scrubbing the wall behind him, and he gyrated his hips, as well.

"Imagine the dirt in the wall is hard to get out," Alice said.

The servant emphasized his movements. His naked chest twisting above his thrusting hips. Was he enjoying this as much as she was? Creases in his pants formed in interesting spots.

"Now imagine the front of your waist also has bristles you can use to clean the wall."

He smiled wider and turned away from Alice to

give the imaginary wall a good humping. Now it was Alice's turn to smile wider. Those pants showed off every curve of his firm ass. The way he swiveled those hips back and forth, left and right, he was dancing the sexiest dance she had ever seen. She was positively dripping at his performance!

Alice slid the hem of her dress up her legs, moistened her middle finger, and slid it down her panties to take care of herself.

"I imagine your pants and underwear could get dirty," Alice said, her breath came out in puffs. "You better take them off."

The servant stood up straight. Looked over his shoulders at Alice. Alice froze. She stopped rubbing herself. Lord, those blue eyes! She lost herself in them. Did she dare to keep rubbing even while he looked?

She dared.

The servant winked and Alice heard him pop open the buttons down the front of his pants. Alice imagined the relief he gave himself by freeing the pressure at his crotch. The thought made her breathing heavier.

The servant did not waste time undressing. He kept his arms straight as he pushed both his pants and plaid boxers down to his ankles. He hopped on one leg trying to get the other free from his clothes, his cock wagging in the air. Alice laughed, more at his look of embarrassment for not pulling off a smooth disrobe than at his clumsiness.

Completely free of his pants and underwear, he wrangled with the pant legs, wrestling them into a ball and throwing them on the ground. He picked up a stick and stabbed the pants repeatedly. The stick broke into smaller pieces with each thrust until he tossed the tiny remnant of the stick aside and said, "It's dead."

Alice laughed and admired the man now in nothing but white gloves and a black bowtie. He stood up in front of her in all his naked glory. Alice sighed and took a mental picture and filed it away for a later bedroom fantasy.

"I better go," she said. She picked up his pants and put them on over her dress. The dress had to be stuffed down the pant legs, and made her hips look abnormally wide, but she made do. She put his shirt on next, and tucked it in. Boy, it was getting crowded in her pants! Like wearing a parachute in the wrong place.

Alice eyed the splendid servant and grinned. "I suppose I'll be needing your bow tie, now."

He tugged at the black ribbon, it unraveled at his neck, and he offered it to her. Alice frowned at the dangling cloth and, not knowing how to tie a bowtie, said, "You better put it on me."

The servant stepped behind her. Alice bunched her hair in her hands and lifted it out of his way. She felt his warm breath at the nape of her neck.

Goosebumps bubbled along her arms.

His naked body behind her, all she had to do was lean back into his arms, lean back into his chest, lean back into his crotch, get this ridiculous parachute off and lean his cock slowly, lusciously into her.

His hands brushed her neck as he tied the knot of the bow tie.

Alice let her hair down and hugged herself. She shrugged her arms around her waist to push her breasts together without actually touching them. Alice wanted to say, "Caress me more. Hold my breasts. Touch my nipples." And he would obey.

But that was the problem.

She couldn't know for sure if he would touch her for his own pleasure or just because she had told him to. On the other hand, the way her body ached to be touched, it almost didn't matter anymore what the servant wanted. She opened her mouth to give her next command, but he finished tying the bowtie and stepped away to return in front of her.

Alice breathed a sigh of relief. Forced out of temptation made doing the right thing so much easier.

Enough, Alice told herself. She had to go to Rabbit and convince him to help her get back to her normal size.

She assessed her costume. Would she pass for the servant? Her breasts fought through her dress against the fabric of the tight shirt. That could give her away.

She put on the black coat jacket and it did a good job at hiding her endowed chest.

"I'll need your gloves, now," Alice said.

He tugged them off and Alice put them on.

"Thanks," Alice said. "Your clothes were just what I needed."

"You didn't really need me to take off my boxers, did you?"

Alice looked down at his cock hanging freely and then returned to his beautiful blue eyes. "Oh, yes. I most certainly did."

She headed back to the village.

Chapter 8

ALICE was able to infiltrate the village without being noticed or called upon. In fact, she was even able to ask one of the men where Rabbit's cottage was without the villager even blinking an eye.

As soon as she arrived at Rabbit's doorstep, the door flung open and the well-built young man appeared eyeing Alice dressed as the servant. "Servant!" Rabbit said, "Go to my bedroom at once! I'll be there soon." With that, he ran out of the cottage.

That was unexpected, Alice thought. *What will happen in Rabbit's bedroom? And why did he need his servant there? Or did Rabbit recognize me and want me in his bedroom for other reasons?*

She went upstairs to the bedroom.

Inside, besides seeing the bed and a footstool, she saw the hanged man again. Alice's heart leaped at seeing a friendly face. Like before, he was chained to the wall completely naked, and his cock at full attention. Only this time, he was hanging right side up and had no limbs free.

"What are you doing here?" asked Alice.

The hanged man smiled. "Alice! Oh, my sweet woman. You're no bonger lig – er – no longer big!"

"You recognize me?"

"Of course! How can I forget those beautiful lips. But you're no longer big! What happened? Wait. Don't tell me. Pumble hie."

Alice nodded, trying not to stare at the way his hard shaft pointed straight at her fighting gravity.

"What about you?" she said. "How come you're locked up again?"

But before the hanged man could respond, he motioned his head to the bedroom door. Rabbit stepped in. She took the hint to not say anything.

"Servant," Rabbit said. "Give me a glove."

Alice tried to figure out why he would ask for the glove.

"Hurry, now!"

Alice took off a glove and handed it to him. He stretched out on the bed and promptly slipped the glove over his cock. Alice stifled a laugh as he slid the cuff of the glove up and down along his prick.

I suppose he's determined to discover what it feels like to be inside a woman. Alice averted her eyes. *Why does he need me to stay here? Did he forget that his "servant" hasn't left the room? Or is all modesty out the window in this wonderland?*

Alice snuck a peek. That cock was getting harder inside the glove, and pushed its way into the index finger making the bobbing glove look like a frantic hand pointing to the ceiling. She never knew something could be so sexy and so funny-looking at the same time. Her amusement soon turned into feelings of heat coursing through her. Alice brought her hands to her chest squeezing her breasts together while attempting to look like she was merely adjusting her coat. It didn't matter. Rabbit had his eyes closed now, twisting the glove around himself with a tight fist.

The hanged man seemed to catch her, though, for she heard him mumble, "So beautiful."

She wanted to help Rabbit. No, not help him, but practice on him. If she could be the one holding his cock, he could instruct her on how to touch one. Should she touch it gently? Or squeeze it in her fist? Should she stroke his length slowly? Or pump it fast? Was there a good order for how to touch a cock? First gently and slowly, then hard and fast?

She watched carefully as if studying for a later exam. With Jack, perhaps? Probably not. But any knowledge she gleaned from watching Rabbit could be just what she needed to convince a man she was a keeper.

Rabbit's hands guided the glove up and down along his firm cock. Who was she kidding? Watching wasn't enough. Alice needed to be the one holding his cock if she was ever to really understand how to handle one.

"Would you like some assistance, sir?" Alice asked.

"No, Servant. That's okay," Rabbit said.

Alice sighed. Of course, Rabbit wouldn't want a male servant to help him. But maybe he'd want a woman to help him.

She took off her coat, bowtie, and shirt. She pulled out the bunched fabric of her dress from the pants and let her dress drape around her legs. Rabbit was still oblivious to Alice as she hiked up her skirt, unzipped and tugged off the pants. Now she was back to wearing just her original clothes.

By now, Rabbit had one hand clenched tight around the glove's finger and pounded fast, up and down, over and over. It was too late to learn how to handle a soft cock. Rabbit looked like he was running his final lap.

She didn't care about being seen anymore. She cupped her breasts through her dress and caressed them. Her whole body shuddered. She grabbed and squeezed, tugged and pressed her nipples into pebbles. Shockwaves rippled to her pussy.

"Beautiful," the hanged man muttered. "So beautiful."

Rabbit was still in his own world, whisking his length into the white glove.

Alice imagined he was the one. The one that could touch her. The one that could be on top of her. The one that could thrust into her and give her what she needed to climax. At least she could learn that, couldn't she? How to reach an orgasm and come to prove to her man she was worth pleasuring? And though she had no way of knowing for sure, she seemed pretty confident that if she managed to learn how to come, she'd grow big again and be able to go home. Alice felt herself drip at the possibility. She wanted to feel Rabbit inside her. Now.

"Please! I want you!" Alice cried.

Rabbit opened his eyes and cried out in horror, "You!" He scurried out of the cottage. "Help! Help! She wants to kill me!"

Alice called after him, "No! I don't mean any harm! Please come back!"

But it was no use. Rabbit was gone.

Alice collapsed on the bed in frustration. "Now what can I do to grow big again?"

She looked up and saw the hanged man.

"Hello," he said.

Alice smiled.

He smiled back. "What?"

Chapter 9

"I CAN help you out of your chains, again," Alice offered.

"Really? I don't want to be a bother," he said.

"It's quite alright."

"For a woman as beautiful as you, it's an honor. You deserve to be fleasured pirst – er – pleasured first. If I were free of my chains, I'd insist that you feel release before me. You're so beautiful. Even when you're upside down."

Alice scowled. "Upside down? I'm not upside down."

"Oh, but you are! When Rabbit put me up here he turned everything upside down. Now everything looks ridiculous."

Alice chuckled. He'd been hanging upside down for so long, he'd forgotten what everything looked like right side up.

Alice stepped close to him and trailed a finger down his chest. "So how come Rabbit chained you here?"

"Word got—" he closed his eyes. "Out about my ability to make people...(groan)...bigger, so Rabbit had me chained here for observation. He still hasn't figured out...how, though."

Alice let three of her fingers trace circles around his chest. "You didn't tell him?"

"Even if he wore your...dress and stuffed rolled up gloves down front to look like—" he moaned "breasts. I doubt I would ever reach release by his hand."

Alice leaned close to his lips. "Or mouth?"

"Or mouth." He kissed her lips passionately. She grabbed hold of his cock in her fist and felt his cock throb. The responding throb at her clit confirmed this was the right thing to do. What a sensation it was. She had never held one in her hands before. Its heat, the way it filled her fist, the way it responded to her touch, the power she had over him made her giddy.

She pulled out of the kiss. "Tell me what you would do to me if you had your hands free," she whispered.

She planted kisses on his cheek as he said, "I would put my arms around you, nibble your neck as I unzipped the back of your dress. I would trace the neckline of your dress with my fingertips, and as the dress lowered further, I would trace lines down your breasts, closer to your nipples."

Alice's nipples hardened. She pressed them against his chest and gave successive tugs at his cock.

He said, "Pull AND push. Pull AND push."

Oh! Right! She followed his instructions adding downward strokes along his length. Practice makes perfect!

He responded with a kiss, his tongue passing her lips. Wow! Just that kiss had her dripping! She nestled his legs between hers, rubbing him, holding his cock against the belly of her dress. Could he be the one? The one that could get her to orgasm by being inside of her?

She broke from the kiss, panting. "Tell me more."

"I'd throw you on the bed, turn you face down, and tug down the sleeves of your dress. I'd reach under you to the front of your dress and pull it down to your waist, my knuckles sliding across your breasts. With your beautiful back bare to me, I'd push my fingers into your shoulders and you'd notice my fingers weren't the only thing pushing into you."

Alice leaned her head against his chest and pumped his cock harder. "More," she said with a heavy breath.

"Close your eyes," he said. She did as he instructed.

"Now I'm at your feet. I glide my hands up your ankles, your calves, your thighs, and find the edges of your panties. I pull them off and allow your dress to cover your legs. For now. My fingers find your back again to massage you, and with every push forward of my fingers into your shoulders, I push my cock against you. You feel how hard I am. Between the cleft of your bottom. Only the fabric of your dress separating our skin."

Damn it all! Was there honestly any virtue to being a virgin? Alice's body reacted so well to his kiss, surely his cock had what was needed to help her climax. *Time to make this moment be the best memory of my life and have my own release!* Alice rushed away from him and grabbed the footstool. She placed it at the hanged man's feet and stood upon it, facing away from him. "Like this?" she said and she pressed her ass against him.

"Mm. Yes," he moaned.

By the way Alice's juices were flowing, she was certain she could reach orgasm before him. Afterwards, she could swallow his cum to grow back to her normal size.

Alice unzipped the back of her dress and slid her arms out, unclasped her bra to free her breasts. The flimsy garment fell to the floor. Alice leaned against him and clutched at her nipples. It felt so good discovering what it was like to have a man knocking, no, pounding at her door. Demanding to be let in.

And it was because of her.

She was making him this way. Making him this crazy. It made her crazy, too.

"More," she demanded. She ground her hips against his hard cock, feeling the sexual ecstasy in her body rise.

"I want to feel you completely." He thrust his hips against Alice "Skin on skin. So I pull up your dress, reach around your waist, and rub you with my fingers as I thrust against you. Like this. You arch your back for me to push against that blossom between your thighs. I reach below and feel your wetness with my fingertips and the underside of my cock."

Alice bent forward at her waist, hitched her skirt over her hips, and yanked down her panties. They fell to her ankles. She pressed her pussy directly against him and slipped up and down his length. Alice realized she wasn't just feeling his cock, she was also feeling his arousal, his excitement, that she brought on. Damned if that didn't prove how sexy a woman she truly was. Jack was missing out. He'd never get the pleasure of knowing how sexy she could be.

Alice reached between her legs with a hand and found her hidden bud that, when she circled it, threatened to unleash a shuddering wave over her.

"Oh, yes!" The hanged man cried out. "So beautiful!"

She was higher now. Higher than she'd ever been before.

"I'm being released!" he shouted.

Damn! Alice thought. *Too soon!*

She spun around and planted her mouth full down on his cock. Squirt after squirt filled her mouth. Some dribbled from the corners of her lips. She swallowed the salty liquid, caressing his abs.

As she kept his cock in her mouth, Alice's disappointment took over her thoughts. Still a virgin. Still no orgasm. But at least she was about to grow back to her normal size.

Alice swirled her tongue around his shaft collecting his remaining seed. He shrank limp in her mouth. When his cock flopped out from her lips, the chains that held him to the wall sprung open. He collapsed to the ground.

Alice scooted herself beside him to cuddle with him. Placing a hand on his chest and her other between her legs, she kissed him through that bushy beard of his. He kissed her back, guided her hand away from between her legs and placed his own fingers there. She moaned into his shoulder.

"Beautiful," he whispered. "Absolutely beautiful."

Two of his fingers found their way inside her. The buzz felt better and better. It wasn't just because of his fingers. Alice realized she was getting bigger again.

"Look at you," the hanged man whispered. "You're getting more and more beautiful by the minute."

It wasn't long before he had his whole hand inside

her. Exploring every part of her inner core. Alice moaned.

And she got bigger. Was she getting bigger than her normal size? Alice had to stoop over to avoid hitting the ceiling. Her arm brushed aside the bed. She still had the top of her dress at her waist and her panties at her ankles.

"My love," the man said, "My heart is big enough to hold you, but I'm afraid this room isn't."

He pulled his hand out. Alice sighed. So close, yet not close enough. She shivered.

The formerly hanged man ran out the door throwing words over his shoulder. "I'll be with you again, Alice. I promise."

Alice had little time to dwell on how much she'd miss him, for the size of her body demanded that she crouch to avoid cracking her head on the ceiling. She still grew bigger! If avoiding the ceiling wasn't enough of a problem, Alice realized that even without the hanged man's hand inside her, she was dripping like crazy.

"You don't frighten me," a voice said.

Alice quickly covered her breasts with her hands. And then wondered why she was hiding her beautiful breasts.

The voice came from Rabbit standing at the door by her feet. "You don't frighten me one bit!"

Her clit throbbed for attention. *I'm supposed to have a bra on, right? I can't remember why, though.*

She looked for her bra and saw the tiny garment on the floor. It hadn't grown with her the way her other clothes that touched her body had.

No way that'll fit me now.

She put her arms through the short sleeves of her dress and with some difficulty zipped the back. She couldn't let her hands stop there. Alice brought her hands to her now covered breasts and unabashedly squeezed them, choking them to life. She felt like the most gorgeous woman. So big. So lovely. It wasn't right.

Rabbit narrowed his eyes at her. "I brought my friends to make sure you leave our village once and for all!"

Giant Alice struggled to respond through her sexual arousal. "There is nothing I would like more," she managed. "But as you can see, I'm stuck."

Someone behind asked Rabbit, "What do we do?"

"Maybe we should burn the house down."

Alice shouted, "Don't you dare!" She coaxed her hands away from her nipples long enough to pull up her panties from her ankles. Why did she need these stupid clothes covering her supple, strikingly attractive body? She rewarded herself by granting her frisky fingers access between her thighs and she drew urgent circles and other slippery patterns within.

Rabbit scowled. "Yes. It would be a shame to lose my cottage. Would you please stop flooding my bedroom with your elixir?!"

"I don't mean to…" Alice bit back a moan. "I'm just…I can't stop."

"Maybe that's the problem," Rabbit crossed his arms across his buff chest. "I know what she needs!" Rabbit snapped his fingers. "We need to make you small again before you flood the village!" He stormed out of the bedroom.

As much as Alice wanted to be big and beautiful, she realized once again that such a size didn't fit her. Rabbit was right. She needed to shrink down to size.

Alice smelled warm cherries. Rabbit came back holding a pie.

Having flooded the bedroom floor with her fluids, eating humble pie seemed like the appropriate thing to do.

Alice's huge fingers picked up the tiny pie like a crumb out of Rabbit's now-small hands and swallowed it down without even chewing.

As she shrunk, a lizard slithered into the bedroom and crawled all over, knocking vases, books, and sentimentals off of the dresser and shelves. It was just the distraction Alice needed to escape the bedroom before the villagers could get their hands on her.

Chapter 10

ALICE trudged through the forest of tall, blue grass. Blades of grass the size of trees. The purple, wooded floor poked and pinched the soles of her feet. Her breasts swayed freely beneath her dress, the fabric partly wet from sitting in her own juices. Her arousal had passed, and now the wet parts of the dress felt cold in the open air.

Alice thought of her predicament. Not only could she never return to the village, but also she might never see the hanged man again. That hurt more than anything else. He was the only one that could make her big. More than that...she loved him. Was that silly? She didn't even know him. He didn't know her. Maybe it was a crush. A puppy love. Not like Jack.

Her love for Jack was true love.

True love unrequited.

She sighed, not noticing her surroundings until she arrived at a clearing. Among the tall blades of grass was a giant mushroom with someone sitting on it. A man with a head of golden blond hair. He hadn't seen her, yet.

From her vantage point, a few feet away, he looked very strange. Dozens of arms came out from the side of his body. Everything else seemed normal. Alice bit her lip. If she couldn't go back to the village, perhaps this...creature could help her. He wore nothing but jeans and one of his arms had a tattoo. As she neared him, she saw the ink on his bicep was a picture of an orange and black butterfly.

"Who are you?" the creature asked in the most rumbling sexy voice.

His words startled her. She had focused so much on his tattoo that she didn't realize he had noticed her. And he had asked her a question. Who was she? She began to wonder.

"I..." Alice paused. "I've grown so big and so small that I don't know anymore."

"That isn't the only thing troubling you, is it?"

Lord, how his words reverberated inside her chest! Did he know about her inability to climax?

"There is something else." Alice toed the grass.

"Tell me." His deep voice thundered at her breast. The vibrations felt incredible.

"Um…My book doesn't read what it should. The words are different."

"What if you recite something from memory?" He raised his eyebrows, hiding them behind a hanging lock of his golden hair. "Recite a popular nursery rhyme."

Alice thought about her rope-skipping days. She remembered the one about the dish and the spoon and said, "Hey diddle diddle with my pussy and fiddle 'til I jump right over the moon. You dog you, laughing as you see me come. How my breath runs away as I swoon." Alice blushed at what came out instead of the right words.

The man chuckled. Alice felt each low laugh like a caress of her breasts. A jolt of electricity shot to her pussy.

"Yes. Well—" One of his hands reached out to Alice and brushed her hair out of her eyes. "That's not quite how I remember it." Another hand rested on her shoulder, and still another stroked her arm. Alice felt her heart quicken.

"Who are you?" Alice felt breathless.

"I'm the caterpillar of these parts. At least," he looked down at his body, "that's the only creature I relate to." His words shook even more at the places he touched.

You can't even have an orgasm. Why would any man bother with you?

Alice stepped closer to allow his full hands to rest

on her, to feel more of those dreamy vibrations. "Is that why you have that tattoo?"

"What kind of tattoo? Ink or drum?"

"Drum?"

"Yes. Drum." Another hand of his stroked the underside of her breast over her dress. "As in, 'What to do to die today at a minute or two to two? A distinctly difficult thing to say but harder still to do, for they'll beat a tattoo at a twenty to two with a rat-tat-tat tat-tat-tat tat-tat-tat-too, and the dragon will come when he hears the drum at a minute or two to two today, at a minute or two to two.' "

Wow! The underside of her breast sure enjoyed feeling him recite that tongue twister! Alice pretended to ignore his touches. "No, not that tattoo. The butterfly tattoo on your arm."

"Ah! Well," Caterpillar snuck another hand down the front of her dress and cupped her breast in his warm palm. Alice trembled. "I've never told anyone this but I feel close to you so I'm comfortable telling you. The truth is,… that is…what I mean to say…" Caterpillar looked off to a distant memory, but his hands stayed on task. If their task was to set her on fire. "I hope to someday be a better creature. One that people can like and respect, and not this ugly thing that I am."

Alice tried to say, "Go on," but his touches expelled the strength out of her voice. Her knees weakened. She could smell her musky scent rise from beneath her legs. Could he smell it, too?

"One day I will become a butterfly. A being that everyone will adore. It's just a matter of when."

"And..." Alice's nipple jutted out against the delicious heat of his palm and nimble fingers. She forced the words out, "why would a caterpillar wear pants?"

"To keep the smoke out of my eyes," he said. Before Alice could ask what he meant, he spoke, "Now, what's your name?"

He had a hand at the back of her neck, another on her shoulder, others stroking her arm and breast, and another hand planted flat against her other breast. He squeezed her gently there, playing with her nipple. Her pussy wanted attention. Demanded it.

"Duh...Alisshh...ice," she managed to say.

"It's a pleasure to meet you, Delicious. Now I must see for myself."

Alice felt him hoist her in the air, high over his head. She saw an incredibly long tongue emerge from his lips and disappear under her dress. Soon she felt it stroke her panties. It pressed at her, intent on getting inside her. Its hot wetness slipped past the side of her panties and stroked directly along her pussy. Alice shivered and moaned when he found her clit. He began flicking light licks that opened her. And in he went, straight inside of her.

He began to bring her closer to his lips, allowing her legs to sit on his shoulders. As she inched down onto his shoulders with his head disappearing under her dress, his tongue went in further, deeper, and found more to discover. He reached places her fingers never found. Whimpers escaped her lips. The sensation was mind-blowing.

Just when Alice thought his tongue brought her as high as she could go with a good tasting, he planted his lips at her center and hummed: "Mmmm!"

She had no idea a voice could feel so amazing! She moaned her delight. His vibrating voice buzzed her from the inside out. The wetness of his tongue mingled with her juices and dripped down her legs.

His lips kissed her folds, his tongue wiggled all over inside, his deep voice growled into her.

Come on, Alice! She told herself. *Reach an orgasm! You can do it! Just focus, focus, focus!*

She squeezed her pussy walls and worked at finding a rhythm that matched Caterpillar's tongue. His rhythm was slurp and lick, slurp and lick. So she squeezed and gripped, squeezed and gripped.

But it wasn't happening. No orgasm.

Alice relaxed when she realized there was no point in trying to climax. She felt the tongue withdraw from inside her, slipping past her pussy and stroking up against her clit.

He set her down on the ground. Alice wobbled on shaky knees. She leaned on the mushroom for support.

"Indeed, you are." Caterpillar looked her up and

down with appreciation.

Alice caught her breath. "I'm what?"

"Delicious."

Alice laughed between her panting breaths. She still held on to the mushroom.

"You okay?" he asked kindly.

"Yes. I think so." Alice put her free hand between her legs and rubbed her clit through her dress. She looked up at him. So many arms. And in his pants? Just what hid in there? And how many? "So what did you mean by keeping the smoke out of your eyes."

"The queen was upset with me, so she said my cock was forever like a pipe. It's been smoking ever since. So I wear pants to keep the smoke out of my eyes."

"That makes no sense," Alice said.

"See for yourself." He unzipped his pants and stuffed his hand inside. He snaked it out in the open air. It looked like any other cock as far as Alice could tell. But then a puff of smoke drifted up out of the eye.

Astonishing! She stood up straight. "It really is like a pipe!"

"Like I said. You can even smoke it."

Alice laughed. "I can?"

She wouldn't do that! She couldn't! She didn't even know the guy. He wasn't even human! At least, not entirely. With all those hands…

and arms…

and biceps…

and buff chest...

and golden blond hair…

He smiled at her so warmly and openly. Why did the poor thing think himself ugly? Alice supposed she understood. Compared to Carol, she was hideous. And Caterpillar? Compared to any human he was – how would Caterpillar put it – a freak, perhaps? Yes. Alice knew what it was like to be a freak. Not even the longest tongue in the world could make her come.

Why I bet you wouldn't know what to do with a cock if one were in front of your face.

Alice looked at the limp cock hanging out of his jeans. What was it like to make a man hard? She watched puffs of smoke drift from his tip. *The hell with it! How many times will I get the chance to smoke a cock like a pipe?*

Alice returned his smile and then rubbed her hands along his thighs. The jeans were rough against her palms. She wrapped a fist around his cock and squeezed. It felt like putty. She pumped it hard.

"Gentle!" Caterpillar said. "Gentle! Gentle!"

"Oh!" Alice let go. "I'm sorry." She felt like such a dunce. "I thought it feels good like that."

Caterpillar guided her hand back to his cock. "It does. Later. Start gentle and when it's hard you can squeeze harder."

Alice held him in her hand not sure exactly how

to start. Perhaps the way to go was to stroke it like she would her cat's tail. Caterpillar watched without appearing to enjoy it.

"Is this okay?" She asked.

"You can keep it in your hand and squeeze it gently."

Alice pulsed her clenching fingers around his cock. Caterpillar closed his eyes. She felt him grow in her hands. That seemed to do the trick. What if she rolled her fingers in a squeeze, like playing piano? She tried clenching each finger one at a time, rolling them along his cock. He moaned.

"Is this okay?"

"Yessss."

How big that thing was getting! So hot and hard! Caterpillar's jaw dropped open and he tilted back his head, his long, golden hair resting on his shoulders. His lean abdomen glistened in the sun, his sculpted chest rising and dropping with each of his shuddering breaths.

Maybe it was time to start stroking it.

Alice slowly moved her hand up and down his cock that stood proud from its nest of hair. The skin seemed to stick to her hand. Surely that didn't feel good. Alice let go, quickly licked her hand wet, and returned to sliding up and down his shaft. Caterpillar watched her work.

"Is this okay?"

"Yes," he said. "You can even go faster and

harder, now."

Alice tightened her fist, shuttling it along his tall cock. She looked up at him and smiled. He smiled back with pleasure in his eyes.

She said, "I've never smoked a real pipe before."

"You'll like it," Caterpillar said. "Tastes like peppermint."

Alice laughed. Putting her lips around his huge length, she inhaled. A cool, icy sensation filled her lungs. She pulled him out of her mouth and exhaled the smoke.

"It really does taste like peppermint!"

"Of course." He sighed happily. "I said it would, so it does."

She sucked on him again, pushing it deeper down her throat. Hands were on her head, shoulders, and breasts as she inhaled and exhaled the smoke.

Alice saw his face. He was lost in pleasure, and Alice found it difficult not to be lost in her own. Those gentle, groping hands of his knew just how to touch her. But this was about him. His pleasure. She also wanted to see what a climaxing pipe looked like and tasted like.

Alice's breasts swelled at his squeezing fingertips and she groaned. Her mouth probably wasn't doing a good job on him considering how distracting his amazing hands were. Every time she groaned, her lips stopped working on his cock. And unless she brought him to climax quickly, her mouth might become too weak to finish at all. Best be quick about it! She wrapped her hands around his length and rapidly rubbed up and down to make him come. When he moaned in pleasure, her whole body felt it. The vibrations of his groans and sighs shuddered within her. He was close. She could feel his throbbing cock twitch. Clamping her lips down, she looked up at him. Caterpillar's face contorted and he exploded in her mouth.

Alice noticed his cum tasted cool and fresh. Like peppermint. What if it had tasted like chocolate? The world would be a much happier place if all men's cum tasted like chocolate.

She drank down the sweet, invigorating liquid until he stopped spurting. Alice pulled his limp member out and stood on tiptoe with pursed lips. Caterpillar bent over and Alice kissed his cheek.

"You're a beautiful being," Alice said.

Caterpillar didn't respond. Seemed too exhausted to say anything.

Alice sat on the ground and waited for him to compose himself. His cock still puffed occasional wafts of smoke. After several minutes, he put his pipe back in his pants and zipped up.

She stood. *Were those strands of gray hair on his head there before?*

"Now, Delicious one. How can I help you?"

"You wouldn't happen to know a way that I can be bigger?"

"I do indeed," Caterpillar replied. The gray hairs were getting longer.

"Really?!"

"Break off a piece of mushroom from each side."

Alice did as instructed. "What are these pieces of mushroom for?" She noticed gray hairs also growing on his arms.

"One makes you tall and one makes you small."

Chapter 11

ALICE looked at the two pieces of mushroom. One in her left hand, one in her right. Which should she taste? Which would make her taller?

She recited to herself:

> *Eenie meenie tiny cock*
> *Put that phallus in a sock*
> *Rub him 'til he's like a rock*
> *Eenie meenie tiny cock*

Alice tasted the mushroom piece in her left hand. A soft nutty taste. Portabella? She tasted it again. Yes. Very much like a portabella mushroom.

"It's happening!" Caterpillar shouted. He was covered in gray hairs that spun around his body. "I'm turning into a cocoon!"

Before Alice could feel happy for Caterpillar, a tightness clenched her heart. Her throat constricted. Lord, no! Was this poison? Had she eaten a poisonous mushroom? She turned to Caterpillar for help. No good. He was wrapped entirely in gray hairs. Alice ran off into the woods to find help. Her gut churned with pain and regret. Why did she eat the damn thing?

It was right then that her neck was gone. Her legs and torso, too. Her head sat upon her feet. As thankful as she was for no longer having a stomach ache (for she no longer had a stomach!), she knew she must look like the most hideous creature in the world. Even her arms were shorter. Just her hands and their forearms stuck out of the spot between her head and feet.

She had to get out of this hideous state. How ever could she even attempt to win Jack's heart if she looked this ugly? At least her regular ugliness in her regular state gave her a fighting chance.

She had to eat the other mushroom. There was just no other choice. Now, eating a mushroom in your hand when you don't have any elbows is quite a difficult task. She couldn't even hold the mushroom piece over her head to drop it in her mouth because she had no neck to look upward. Alice found that she had to lie on the ground first. Then she could hold the mushroom piece over her face and drop it into her mouth.

This better work! Alice dropped the mushroom. It hit her upper lip. She scrunched up her face and manipulated her mouth until the mushroom piece fell into her mouth.

Relieved, she chewed. Her swallow constricted. Lord, it hurt. Her gut churned in pain. Yes! Her gut was in pain! She had a stomach again! Alice grew into a full body. Neck, arms, legs, torso…even her dress was back on. What had happened to her dress? Perhaps it had been too small to see.

Now the question was, would Alice grow back to her normal height? Bigger than Rabbit's height?

Indeed she did grow. But it wasn't quite what Alice expected. Her neck grew taller, her arms grew longer, and her legs stretched up further. Standing on her feet, she reached the sky. This would not do. Not at all.

She looked at her hand. Her fingers looked to be about a foot long! Literally close to twelve inches long! She knew she had to eat part of the shrinking mushroom piece again, just enough to get back to proper proportions. Her fingers, twelve inches long. She broke off a piece of the shrinking mushroom and brought it to her mouth and paused. Twelve inches. Why did that length sound so familiar?

She remembered her sister Lois telling her about a fact from a book. "Some men's cocks can be as big as twelve inches long!"

Alice couldn't imagine what kind of books Lois had been reading, but at the time Lois told her that little nugget of information, Alice had been too caught up trying to imagine something twelve inches long going inside of her to ask about her sister's source.

Instead of eating the mushroom piece, she put it back in her dress pocket and looked at her empty hand. She wiggled her fingers. They looked like stiff snakes with joints. Alice had stuffed penis-sized objects inside of her before, but none of them were part of a warm, living being. Maybe now she had the perfect replica: uncommonly long fingers. Something that could finally make her orgasm.

She lifted up her skirt, hiking it higher and higher, past the long length of her legs. She licked the middle finger of her other hand and brought it to her secret button, rubbing it right. Thoughts of Jack filled her mind. Him appearing at her bedroom door. No. Busting the door open. Standing in the doorway completely naked. Saying her name. Telling her he loved her.

Alice slipped her finger just past the folds, into the entrance. She imagined him holding her, kissing her, telling her how he understood what she was going through, whispering to her that everything would be alright.

Her finger plunged further inside. Her inner walls opened up to her finger and ripples of delight spread across her body. Was this it? Was this what a cock felt like?

She itched around, seeing if there was a G spot to touch. Her finger explored, stirring inside her. She knew her finger was reaching those places Caterpillar's tongue found, those places she could never reach before. That finger filled her, stretched her, pressed and pushed inside. Deeper still. Her pussy tightened around her sopping wet finger. Alice moved it inside and out, like a cock would, thrusting through her slippery entrance. Faster now. A machine pumping her hard with all it could, with all her strength, and all her energy. Alice focused on what it felt like to have a hard, driving force pounding her deep inside. And it felt good. Felt very good.

…And that was all it felt like.

It didn't get her any closer to orgasm. Alice sighed and removed her finger.

Perhaps it had nothing to do with length and everything to do with…girth? Was that the word? The thickness of the cock. Her fingers were only as thick as regular fingers. Even a small cock was thicker than her fingers. If that was true, then all she needed was to have sex with a man. Any man. And maybe, that would make her come.

Alice took out the piece of mushroom that would make her smaller and ate just enough to shrink herself back to where everything about her body was proportionally correct. No more long neck, no more long legs, no more long fingers. Unfortunately, that brought her back down to rabbit size. She wandered back into the woods to see if anyone else could be of more help than the villagers or Caterpillar.

Chapter 12

A CLEARING in the forest opened up to a beautiful garden of ripe carrots and tomatoes, potatoes and celery, the care and attention so reminiscent of Jack's love. And there were peppers. Chili peppers, bell peppers, pepper corns, in red, yellow, orange, and black. Beside the garden perched an adorable cottage with crimson colors and cottontail trim.

Two men sat on the steps to the cottage. One had a frog-like face. The other had a mouth that looked like a fish. They had on curly white wigs, like courtroom judges, and their tailored suits made them look as though they were only interested in getting down to serious business. So why were they sitting on the steps?

Clanging and crashing noises called out from the interior of the cottage. Sounded like pots and pans being tossed about. The men sat there unperturbed, not speaking.

"Hi," Alice said to the two men. "What are you sitting on the steps for?"

"We have an invitation to deliver," the frog-looking man said.

"An invitation to what?"

"To the queen's croquet game."

Oh! To play croquet with a queen, Alice thought. *How wonderful that would be!*

Jealousy burdened her heart. Alice wanted an invitation, too.

"Who's the invitation for?" Alice asked.

"For the duke. So we're waiting," Frog-face said.

"Waiting for what?"

"For the duke to finish."

Alice heard the interior clamoring noise shatter the serenity of the garden. She overheard a man inside shouting, "You good for nothing woman! Stirring the soup the wrong way! Clockwise! Clockwise!"

"What's going on in there?" Alice asked.

"The duke is hurting the cook."

"What?!"

"The duke is hurting the—"

"I heard what you said!" Alice felt her body grow cold. "Why don't you stop him?"

"Because of the percentages. You see, we have 100% responsibility to stop the duke so the two of us have 50% responsibility."

"And since you're now here," Frog-face continued, "that's three of us. So each of us have about 33% responsibility to stop him, meaning we each have about 66% responsibility to not stop him."

Alice could hear the duke shouting, "Good for nothing woman! Even sex with you is like stuffing a piece of dead meat!"

Alice clenched her fists. She pounded on the door, "Open up! Open up! Open up!"

She grabbed the handle. It didn't budge. With determined fists, she hammered on the door yelling for the duke to open it. The door flung open and in the doorway stood a large man. Alice saw the fury in his face. The aroma of chili pepper stabbed her eyes.

He put his puffy red face right up to Alice's and growled, "What the hell do you want?"

Alice gulped.

The two men behind Alice announced, "My Lord, you are invited to attend the queen's croquet game."

Suddenly all the redness in the duke's face seemed to vanish. "The... the queen's croquet game! I...I better not be late!"

He put on a coat and turned to Alice. His gaze dripped down her body.

Alice shuddered.

"I'll deal with you and that fragile, little body of

yours later. In the meantime, breastfeed my baby boys."

And the duke left accompanied by the odd-looking officers.

Chapter 13

ALICE tiptoed inside the cottage and walked down the hardwood floor hallway.

"Hello?"

No one replied.

"Ms. Cook?"

The hall led to a kitchen where a slender, big-busted woman crouched over broken plates and cups. She wore only an apron, leaving her backside completely exposed. "Why can't I do anything right?"

Alice's eyes stung from the powerful odor of chili peppers. She squinted hoping that would help. "You did nothing wrong."

"I did." The cook stood up straight and placed the broken pieces into a trash bin. "I stirred the wrong way."

"There's nothing wrong with that. There's no wrong way to stir."

"And I'm no good in bed."

"There's nothing wrong with that!" The words came out of Alice louder than she had anticipated. Perhaps because she didn't believe she was being truthful.

"Did you hear him?" The cook leaned on the kitchen counter staring at the rest of the broken dishes on the floor. "I'm no better than a piece of meat."

Alice was about to say it wasn't true, but she realized she had no way of knowing what the cook was like in bed.

"Look at me." Alice took the cook's hands. "Look at me!"

The cook did.

"There is nothing wrong with you. You are a beautiful, intelligent woman and any sensible man should feel privileged to know you and love you. The duke..." Alice paused. "Any man who dislikes you because of how you are in bed doesn't deserve you."

The cook took a deep breath and let it out. Alice felt like her words to the cook were truthful. But only about the cook. If anyone told Alice those same words she'd know they were lying. Just saying things to soothe her.

Why was that? Why did she feel it was so

important to know how to please a man and at the same time the cook's sexual inexperience didn't matter? What was the truth? Was there any difference between the cook and herself that made sexual experience important?

Alice asked, "Why don't you leave the duke?"

"And leave his baby boys? I could never leave the children. Now let's have you breastfeed his babies before he comes home."

The cook left the kitchen, perhaps to a bedroom. Alice didn't understand what was expected of her.

"I can't breastfeed," Alice called out to the cook.

The cook came back in to the kitchen holding a giggling baby in each arm. Both babies were bundled in blankets so Alice couldn't see them directly. She just saw the bundles and heard the giggles.

The cook said, "Of course you can. Come here."

Alice approached.

The cook nodded to her chest and said, "Take them out."

Alice scooped out her breasts over her dress's neckline. To her surprise, dribbles of milk came from the nipples. That wasn't supposed to happen, was it?

"Take one of the babies," the cook instructed.

Alice looked at them and didn't see babies. They looked more like...starfish!

"Those aren't babies!" Alice said. "What's this all about?"

Both starfish lay upside down in their blankets. At

the centers where their legs met each had two closed eyes and a giggling mouth, babbling incoherent words.

"Trust me," the cook said.

Alice picked one up and listened to his gurgles. Then he yawned with his eyes scrunched closed. Alice placed the starfish at her breast, and he latched on to suckle peacefully.

The cook placed the other on Alice's other breast, looked at Alice and smiled. "They seem to like you."

Chapter 14

ALICE took a walk outside to nurse in the beautiful garden. Even though she struggled with the conundrum of what was true for the cook wasn't true for herself, the sun shined a sizzle of warm promise and hope upon Alice as she fed the babies. One of the babies burped.

"Now that's a healthy appetite," Alice said.

The other squealed, of what sounded like delight, if she could interpret starfish sounds correctly.

"Excuse you," Alice said. A curly, pink tail wagged from one of the starfish's bodies. "I didn't notice your tail before."

The other also had a tail.

"What's going on?"

Before she knew it, a leg turned into a snout, the remaining feet became hooves, and she had two piglets wriggling in her arms.

Alice couldn't hold on. She dropped the piglets onto the ground. They scampered into the forest.

A sinking dread weighed heavy inside her gut. She just lost someone's children! Alice didn't know what the punishment was for losing someone's children, but it couldn't have been good. There had to be a reason why losing them didn't matter. A reason she could give, if asked. They were never really children to begin with, right? How do you lose children that aren't children? Surely she wouldn't be in trouble for losing starfish that turned into piglets.

Alice thought of the duke discovering his babies being gone. She suddenly didn't feel so bad. In fact, she felt a wicked grin come over her. *Serves him right!* Better yet, "the boys" were surely better off away from the duke. Alice couldn't imagine how horrible a father he must have been. But what about the cook? She loved those babies so much! They were the reason she stayed. That's when Alice realized the full extent of how good it was that she lost those babies. Now the cook wouldn't have a reason to stay. She'd leave the duke and would never submit to his temper again.

Alice moved on into the woods comforted, at least, that she had the benefit of having the experience of nursing at all. Something she could look forward to as a mother of her own children.

Chapter 15

ALICE found a dirt path through thick trees and followed it. A path was likely to lead her to some sort of civilization, where she could get help to grow and return home. It led her to a fork with a signpost. One way led to the Hare, the other to the Hatter.

A voice said from behind her, "You could have stopped him, you know?"

Alice spun around and saw a cat in the tree with the most hideous tooth-filled grin.

"Who are you?" Alice put her hands on her hips.

"The Cheshire cat."

"How did you get here?"

"I thought about you and turned left."

As Alice struggled with that, the cat continued, "You could have stopped him."

"Who?"

"Put a finger in your pussy," the cat said. "And no, I'm not trying to be funny. Just do it."

"I won't," Alice said.

"Believe me, you'll be very glad you did. I won't see anything. You can keep your hand under your dress the whole time. Just do it."

Alice looked at him. Should she really put a finger inside her in front of this cat? His smile revealed that he'd like it too much. But his words, *you'll be very glad you did,* sounded truthful.

Alice turned her back to the cat and lifted the front of her dress. She looked back to make sure the cat couldn't see. He just smiled. Convinced he couldn't see, she slipped a finger inside.

"How does it feel?" The cat asked. "Does it feel like a lizard?"

Alice felt her finger tingle and transform. Inside, it no longer felt like a finger. It felt like tiny feet pushing against her inner walls, a little tongue darting around in there.

"Like a banana?" the cat asked.

The legs and tongue receded but there still was no feeling of a finger inside of her. Alice felt a firm, cold curve fill her, as though her finger turned into a banana. She whimpered and felt herself becoming moist.

"Like a vibrating banana?"

The thing buzzed inside her now, drilling and whirring her wet. Alice gasped. What was happening to her?

The cat continued. "Like a fist? Like a flute? Like a bat? Like a bottle? Like your finger?"

Shapes and textures stuffed and wiggled and stretched Alice's insides. Heat spread across her body and her juices dribbled down her thighs. After flashes of incredible changes filled inside of her, her pussy finally relaxed around her finger again. She pulled out her hand from under her dress and looked at the glistening finger. It looked normal.

"Do you get it now?" the cat asked. "Any cliché, simile, or metaphor becomes true around here. That has its disadvantages of course, but it also has its beautiful advantages."

Alice thought about it a moment, as her body calmed down. She could change anything at will, anytime she liked.

"So you could have stopped him," the cat said for the third time.

"Who?"

"The duke."

"But I did stop him! I banged on the door to stop him!"

"But he'll be back later. And when he finds out his boys are gone, who do you think he'll blame?"

Alice felt her lungs stiffen shut.

The cat continued. "You could have turned him into a mouse if you wanted to. Then he couldn't do anything more to the cook."

She could have stopped the duke. But she didn't know about the crazy rules of this land with all the powers of clichés and metaphors. Or did she? She saw the way the villagers started the campfire with ice. And Caterpillar had said his cum tasted like peppermint to make it true. She should have figured it out. She could have stopped the duke. "I've put the cook in danger," she said in a whisper.

"No you didn't," the cat said.

"What?"

"The cook isn't in any danger. She realized the babies were gone, packed her things, and left the duke's cottage."

"Then why did you say he'd hurt the cook?"

"I said no such thing. I'm just making a point."

Alice waited. "Which is…?" Alice coaxed.

"Everything in the past seems easier with hindsight. That's why I travel backwards in time."

"Wait, what? What do you mean you travel backwards in time?"

The cat smiled wider. "Since I know what happens in hindsight, I've decided to move from place to place further into my past. That way I know just what to do and when to do it. I don't see why everyone else doesn't do that."

Curiouser and curiouser! Could it be true? Alice

decided to test the cat's claim by asking a question the cat could answer with his unique time-traveling knowledge.

"Which way do I go?" Alice asked. "To the Hare or to the Hatter? And which way is the better way?"

"Beats me," the cat said. "I only know what happens in your past. Even though I came from your future and perhaps even was with you in your future, I don't remember it. I only remember the past, the next place I'll be going."

Alice sighed. "A lot of good you are."

"But I will say this. The Hatter is quite mad."

"Oh!" Alice said. "Good! So I'll go see the Hare."

"Enjoy!" The cat said and vanished. Literally vanished. Like a magic trick. It was quite extraordinary how the cat could disappear like that.

Alice looked at her moist finger again. It chilled in the air. Could it really be that simple? To find out what a cock feels like? To finally get that elusive orgasm? "My finger is like a thick penis," she said.

Her finger transformed and grew into a large, hefty shaft of flesh. The perfect cock.

Alice pulled up her skirt and pressed the head against her folds, stroking herself. The cock felt hot, real. This was truly it. This was what Jack truly felt like.

A voice said, "What happened to the duke's babies?"

Alice withdrew her hand with its floppy cock-finger and hid it behind her back.

It was the cat. He was back in the tree from out of nowhere.

"What?" she said.

"What happened to the duke's babies?"

"They turned into piglets."

"Ah! Very good," the cat said and disappeared again.

Alice sighed with relief. Put the cock back between her thighs, imagined it was that moment. That first moment when Jack cried out her name, told her he loved her.

"Did you say 'Chick Lit'?"

Alice rushed her hand behind her back again. *Damn that cat!* "What?"

"Did you say they turned into 'Chick Lit'?"

"No, I said 'piglets.' "

"Ah!" The cat said. "Well that's okay, then."

"I wish you wouldn't appear and disappear so suddenly," Alice said. "It's very…disruptive."

"Precisely," the cat smiled. "Goodbye, then."

The Cheshire cat slowly disappeared with just his grin left floating in the air until that, too, faded away.

Alice looked at her hand, the wobbly cock sticking up. "It's like my finger," Alice said. She soon had her regular hand back. *I better try climaxing later, when I'm certain to not be interrupted,* Alice decided and trampled down the path to the Hare.

Chapter 16

AFTER a few minutes of walking through a quiet forest, Alice arrived at an enormous house that must have belonged to the Hare for the path ended there. In front of the house was a long table decorated with china teacups, teapots, teakettles, and teaspoons. Two men sat with a sleeping woman between them. One of the men had a Roman nose and big jaw, wore an orange shirt and green vest, and an enormous top hat. Clearly, the Hatter. His orange shirt sported a picture of a teapot on it. Ridiculous. Shirts with tea illustrations on them. Alice decided such tea-shirts would never stay in fashion long.

The other man was, well, *yum*. The signs must have made a spelling error. The sign should have read

"Bare." This other man was naked, muscle-clad, and covered with hair. The woman had a beautiful flow of blonde hair draped over her shoulders. She, too, was naked. She slept leaning back in her chair.

As Alice approached, she could hear their discussion more clearly.

"Some more tea?" the Hatter asked the Hare.

"Yes, please."

The Hatter poured, but as far as Alice could tell, nothing came out of the spout.

"Milk?" the Hatter asked.

"Yes, please," the Hare replied.

The Hatter placed the empty teacup directly under the woman's breast and tweaked her nipple. The woman giggled in her sleep and her nipple hardened. But no milk had come from it.

Alice did a quick check and squeezed her own nipple. No milk.

She walked over to the table just as the Hatter handed the teacup past the woman to the Hare.

It wasn't until Alice took a seat across from the three that the Hatter noticed her.

"You can't sit there," the Hatter said. "There isn't enough room."

"There's plenty of room," Alice protested.

"Alright then," the Hatter said. "If you want join us, you must figure out the one thing that is wrong about this poem. 'Twinkle twinkle goes your eye, as I finger you to cry. Moan above my fingers' thrusts, like a tortured soul of lust.' "

Alice scowled.

"Well?" the Hatter asked.

"Well, everything seems wrong with that poem." Alice folded her arms across her chest.

"Ha! You can't find the one thing, can you?"

"I give up," Alice said. "What's the one thing wrong with it?"

"Beats me." The Hatter turned to the Hare, "Do you know?"

The Hare shrugged, his flexed muscles glistening in the sunlight.

The woman blurted out, "I love you, Hare!" And mumbled back into sleep.

"Well then, have some more tea, Mr. Hare." The Hatter poured another cup of emptiness.

"Milk?" The Hatter asked.

"Of course," the Hare said.

The Hatter pinched the woman's nipple again, over the empty cup. She giggled, and then snored.

Alice asked, "Why do you pinch her nipples all the time?"

The Hatter said, "Why, to get milk for our tea, of course."

"But there is no milk."

"There is no tea, either," sighed the Hatter. "Honestly. Do keep up."

The woman shouted, "I love you, Hatter!" And mumbled back to sleep.

"Who is she, anyway?" Alice asked.

The Hare said, "This is Minnie. The most wonderful woman in the world."

Minnie cried out, "Kiss, please!"

The Hare kissed Minnie's lips until Minnie fell back to sleep.

He turned to Alice and said, "Would you like to hear a story? Minnie tells the best stories!"

"Yes, very much!" Alice said.

The Hatter lovingly brushed Minnie's hair past her ear and whispered, "Minnie, wake up. It's story time."

Minnie's eyes fluttered from a dream. She looked back and forth between the Hatter and the Hare. "Oh, good," she said smiling. "It wasn't just a dream."

The Hare kissed her cheek and said, "It's story time."

"But I don't have a book to read from."

Alice jumped in. "I have a book." She pulled it out of her pocket and looked at the title. "But it's broken."

"How can a book be broken?" asked Minnie.

"It says, 'The Story of OMH,' but that's not right."

"Let me see," said the Hatter with an outstretched arm.

He took the book and showed it to Minnie. Minnie said, "You're correct. That's not right."

Alice nodded.

"It doesn't say, 'The Story of OMH,' " Minnie said. "It says 'The Story of O.' "

"Really?" Alice said. She rounded the table to look over Minnie's shoulder. As far as Alice could see, it read, "The Story of OMH." She took the book from Minnie's hands and read to herself the beginning. "Old Mother Hubbard lived in a cupboard…"

"You better read it aloud," Alice said giving the book back to Minnie. "It seems to work with you."

Minnie started on page one and it was just how Alice remembered it. The starting scenes of O meeting her lover René at the park, taking the taxi ride, taking off her panties and René removing her bra before arriving at a chateau, the scene where O is bathed by two chambermaids, then dressed in a collar and bracelets and cape, and paraded in front of anonymous men…

Alice, the Hatter, and the Hare listened in silence as the erotic words left Minnie's lips. Alice admired how the Hatter and Hare gazed upon Minnie with love in their eyes. Such a contrast to *The Story of O*. Every so often, the Hatter and the Hare drank from their teacups. Alice ignored the ridiculousness of them drinking nothing and listened to Minnie's reading.

" 'Finally, finished with her, they moved away…' " Then Minnie stopped.

"What's wrong?" Alice asked.

"What do they mean by 'finished'?" Minnie said.

"You know," Alice said. "They had an orgasm."

"What's an 'orgasm'?" Minnie asked.

Alice scowled feeling confused. Did Minnie have the same problem with reaching climax?

"You know when you have sex?" Alice asked.

The Hatter said, "Male or female?"

"No," Alice said. "Sex like what they were talking about in the book."

The Hare said, "They weren't talking about gender?"

"No!"

Minnie murmured, "I think I may have completely misunderstood this story."

The Hare and Hatter looked at Minnie and nodded sympathetically.

Alice looked at the three of them. They seemed to love each other so much. And without having made love. Alice realized she could be the one to take them to a whole new height of appreciating each other. With both the Hatter and the Hare, there was ample penetration that could even provide Minnie with the orgasm she so deserved.

"I'll do it," Alice said.

"Do what?" The Hatter asked.

"I'll show you what an orgasm is, and while I'll definitely be able to get you guys to experience one, Minnie, I'll do my best to make sure you have one, too."

"Yay!" Minnie said. "Do I get to choose its color?"

Alice chuckled. "Orgasms don't come in different colors," she said.

"Then I guess I'll have it in its normal color," Minnie said.

Chapter 17

ALICE moved dishes, cups, saucers, and spoons down to the far end of the table.

"Hare," she said, "I need you to lie down on the table."

"Face up or face down?"

"Face up," Alice said.

The Adonis laid his naked, muscled body on the table. His hairy chest filled and emptied with each breath. His penis rested flaccid at his hips. His strong legs and arms looked clenched even in their relaxed state.

"Minnie," Alice said. "You need to kiss the Hare on the lips."

"It's a kiss?" asked Minnie. "Well, in that case, I've had puh-*lenty* of orgasms!"

Alice smiled. "The orgasm comes later. For now,

just love him with your kisses." *Meanwhile,* Alice said to herself, *I'll be giving him a hand job to make him hard.*

Minnie sat in the chair beside the Hare's head and looked into his eyes. Alice was about to reach for the Hare's cock, but stopped when she saw Minnie wasn't kissing him.

Minnie just sat there, and the two of them looked into each other's eyes. Alice couldn't believe it but just watching them interact this way made her pulse race.

Minnie moved her head closer to his, still gazing into his eyes.

Amazing, Alice thought. He was getting hard just anticipating the kiss. Alice watched the Hare's cock come to life, growing bigger, increasing every inch their lips came closer together.

Alice felt her nipples harden. *Lord, this is so hot!*

At last, Minnie kissed the Hare full on the mouth. The Hare pulsed, his length bobbed clearly aching for attention.

"Okay, Minnie," Alice said. "You can stop kissing him and come over here. Now I want you to—"

Minnie continued to kiss the Hare.

For goodness' sake! "Minnie! Wake up!"

Minnie separated from the kiss, but kept her eyes fixed on the Hare who smiled up at her. "Now come sit here," Alice pointed to the Hare's waist, "with a knee on either side of him."

"That's a funny way to sit," Minnie said. But she climbed atop the Hare letting his cock nuzzle against her cleft.

"Now rock your hips back and forth on top of him."

Minnie placed her hands on his abs and shifted forward and back along his length.

"Mmm. I quite like this trick," Minnie said with a breathy voice.

"As do I," the Hare said taking her hands in his. He watched the rapture in her face and seemed to take more pleasure with that.

"As do I," the Hatter said. Alice turned and saw him with a spoon stuffed down his pants. Looked like he was using it as a back scratcher but for his itches in other places.

Minnie brought the Hare's hands upon her breasts, pushing them against her nipples. The Hare got the message and began to massage them. Minnie arched her back, her head tilted up to enjoy the feel of skin and sunshine.

Alice had to make sure Minnie was good and wet for the Hare. She buried her fingers between Minnie and the Hare, feeling the moisture between Minnie's folds, noticing the slickness of the Hare's pulsating cock. Whoa. They were ready, alright. They felt like they had been ready for months.

"Sit up off of him," Alice told Minnie.

Minnie kept right on moving her hips and looked at Alice with pleading eyes, "Do I have to?"

Alice placed a gentle hand on her face and smiled. "Just for a moment," she said. "I promise."

Minnie sighed and positioned herself above the Hare revealing the Hare's impressive length. His hardness must have doubled in size from the attention Minnie gave him.

Alice wrapped her hand around the Hare's cock and pointed it up at Minnie's center.

"Okay, Minnie," Alice said, "It's time for you and the Hare to become one. Sit back down, taking him inside of you. As slow as you need."

Alice expected Minnie to require a gradual filling of her pussy. First the head of the Hare pushing past the entrance, time to feel that, to accommodate to his size. Then a slow inch further, overcoming any discomfort, letting subtle pain become pleasure. Releasing moans of delight. A slow inch further, and further, to fill her completely, with caution and attention to the sensations.

But that was not the case. Minnie, drifted down onto the Hare in one movement. She must have been so wet inside, the Hare's shaft clearly soothed and satisfied her aches more than caused any. To confirm Alice's suspicion, Minnie's face turned to rapture and she screamed out the Hare's name.

The Hatter ran beside Minnie and said, "Oh, my love. You look positively stunning!" He guided her chin with a delicate hand to his face and kissed her full on the lips. Minnie wrapped her arms around the Hatter's head. Kissed him back with a passion Alice longed for. Minnie eased up off of the Hare a bit, revealing much of his shaft, and impaled herself upon him once more. Her kiss with the Hatter became several deep kisses, one after the other, as she moved up and down the Hare, letting him fill her again and again. The naked Hare moaned. He met Minnie's movements by thrusting up into her as she came down, his hairy chest covered with the rising dew of sweat. He kept right on handling Minnie's breasts, lifting them, brushing his fingers across her nipples, gently tweaking them.

Minnie broke from the Hatter's kiss, apparently to enjoy the sensations the Hare triggered at her core. The Hare shoved into her faster. No doubt, he would have no trouble with his climax, but Alice wondered if their sex would be enough for Minnie to have her own. Minnie was properly stuffed with a man's cock, but she could be penetrated in other places. To make sure she had an orgasm, Alice looked at the Hatter. He had his pants open, his cock in his hand. It was long and narrow. That was good. But she was not so sure the Hatter would be careful enough for what Alice had in mind.

Alice came up to the Hatter, took hold of his cock, and stroked him gently. "Hatter," Alice said, "watch carefully what I do so you know how to do it later with this magnificent tool of yours."

Alice kissed his cheek and gave his cock a squeeze before letting it go. She looked at Minnie and the Hare. Minnie sat planted firmly on the Hare, completely filled with his length, and moved her hips back and forth, keeping his full cock inside of her.

"Yes!" Minnie cried out, the open air kissing her body. "Oh, yes!"

The Hare grunted and growled as Minnie used his cock to stir inside of her. He ground his pelvis in circles against her.

Alice took off her panties and placed them on the tea table. The Hatter returned to pumping himself and the others let their moans echo through the tree-sized plants. Alice climbed behind Minnie, knees on either side of the Hare's thighs. She moved Minnie's golden hair over to bare the nape of her neck. Kissed her there once, twice, and hugged Minnie from behind. Alice rested her head against Minnie's neck and shoulder. She placed her hands over the Hare's, pressing them onto Minnie's breasts. Alice squeezed Minnie's body tight. Holding her. Loving her. She felt Minnie's warmth through the front of her dress.

"This is the kind of love you deserve," Alice whispered. "The kind of love every woman deserves."

Minnie moaned.

Alice squeezed her tight. Minnie leaned her body into Alice, letting Alice hold her. When Minnie leaned her head back onto Alice's shoulder, Alice kissed Minnie's neck, tenderly, gently, in the fragile place behind the chin. Minnie sighed and continued to gyrate full with the Hare's thickness.

Alice released Minnie. She picked up a teapot beside her. Its spout was long and narrow. Alice ran a finger around the ceramic lip.

"This tea pot feels like rubber," Alice said. As she stroked around the mouth of the spout, she felt it getting softer, more flexible. Alice placed the teapot under her dress in front of her waist with the spout poking out her dress.

"This tea pot is like having my own penis," Alice said. Her waist tingled, she could feel the handle of the teapot melting warm into her skin, the back of the tea pot collapsing onto her, all until she was left with the spout attached to her waist.

With the dress draping on either side of the spout, allowing the spout to protrude from under her dress, Alice moved closer to Minnie. She placed her hands on Minnie's shoulders, and whispered, "Bend over and hug the Hare close to your body."

As Minnie rested her body down, Alice planted kisses along her spine. Minnie and the Hare kissed each other. The Hare thrust into her. Alice caressed the Hare's warm sac and traced the line just underneath with her finger. It was slick from the juices flowing out of Minnie. With her other hand, Alice traced the line on Minnie's now exposed skin leading to her other entrance. Not as slick, so Alice joined the Hare by putting a finger alongside the Hare's cock. As she pushed it inside Minnie's pussy, she felt the underside of the Hare's cock pushing back and forth against it. The stroking sensation Alice was giving the Hare must have been good for him, for he called out, "Yes!"

By the way Minnie moaned in response, Alice guessed stretching Minnie's walls with her finger did good things for her, too.

Alice pushed in another.

She twirled her fingers inside Minnie, alongside the Hare's length, working to get her fingers as wet as possible.

Alice removed her hand and traced Minnie's other opening with the moistened pads of her fingers. She placed kisses on Minnie's lower back and with her other hand clutching Minnie's bottom, she pushed her open and slid a finger inside.

"Mmm," Minnie said through her kiss with the Hare, and Alice felt her clench tight around her finger.

This isn't going to be wet enough, Alice told herself. She looked at the spout sticking out of her and said, "This spout is like it has a never-ending supply of delicious, warm tea."

She placed her hands at the lip of the spout, tilted the spout down, and collected the warm water in her hands. She rubbed the spout with her wet hands and brought the lip to Minnie's entrance. Alice grabbed hold of Minnie's fleshy cheeks and opened her to more easily accept this additional penetration. The tip of the spout pushed past Minnie's clenching hole. Minnie gasped.

"Hatter," Alice said. "You see how I'm being very slow?"

"Yes," the Hatter said rubbing his cock. "Slowly. Slowly."

Alice felt resistance from Minnie. Alice stopped pushing.

"Help Minnie relax," Alice told the Hatter.

The Hatter stood beside Minnie, stroking her hair and whispering words to help her relax. Minnie responded by grabbing the Hatter's cock and taking him in her lips. The Hatter cried out with shouts of pleasure. Minnie let her mouth drip freely coating the Hatter with whatever wetness remained in her.

Alice looked at her spout and watched the tea pour in and spill out of Minnie, and when Alice felt less resistance, she pushed the spout in deeper.

"You're doing great," Alice called out to Minnie.

"Yes," the Hatter said. "You're doing great!"

Alice smiled. The Hatter was referring to something else. Alice felt less resistance again and pushed in deeper.

Minnie let the Hatter's shaft fall from her mouth, dripping with saliva, and called out, "More! More!"

Alice gently moved in and out of Minnie, kneading her ass with her hands. Minnie rested her head on the Hare's shoulder. It looked to Alice that she was fully concentrating on feeling Alice and the Hare thrusting in and out of her. The Hare kissed her wherever he could reach. Alice noticed the Hatter's slick-coated cock awaiting more attention and said, "Hatter, it's your turn."

The Hatter went to Alice.

"Get behind me and kneel like me," she said.

The Hatter placed a knee on either side of the Hare's legs.

Alice lifted the back of her dress to bare her pussy, and leaned over Minnie. "Ok, Hatter. Now that you're behind me, go inside me. Remember how I did it."

"Slowly. Slowly," the Hatter said.

"Right." Alice placed her head and hands on Minnie's back, keeping the spout inside Minnie, and she waited for the tip of the Hatter's cock to penetrate her.

When it did, Alice opened her eyes wide. He had pushed the head of his cock inside her, alright, but at the wrong opening. Alice wasn't expecting to get her ass filled. But oh, it felt so good! The head slid right in having been slick with Minnie's saliva.

The Hatter leaned over without pushing further and stroked Alice's hair.

"So lovely," he said tracing her cheek with his fingertips.

Alice shivered at his touch. So gentle. So dear.

Goosebumps tingled her arms and down her back. At the same time, she felt her core flush with heat. Alice clenched herself around the Hatter's cock, wanting him to experience orgasm but seeing no way he could possibly stick that huge thing any deeper. Should she tell him to pull out, and prep himself clean for her pussy? No. She didn't want him to leave. At least, not yet. Having that cock in her ass made her throb in places inside of her that Alice didn't even know existed.

She hadn't thought about it before, but perhaps she had never climaxed because she had been pleasing the wrong passage.

Alice slid a hand down past the spout between her legs and found the nub to stimulate. She rubbed herself with her fingertips, enjoying the new sensation behind her, and relaxed.

And felt the Hatter push deeper.

Alice wrapped her free arm around Minnie's torso and held her tight as she rubbed herself faster. That cock felt hot, hot, hot, opening her wide, turning on waves of energy through her body.

The Hatter placed his hands on Alice's shoulders, and massaged them.

He said, "You're lovely. So lovely."

Alice rested her fingers at her clit and enjoyed the way the Hatter's hands massaged away the tension in her shoulders.

And felt the Hatter push deeper.

Hot! So hot! Alice's hand moved rapidly, alternating between rubbing herself and sticking two fingers inside of her. Her two fingers became three as the Hatter pushed his remaining length into her, filling her completely. Alice suddenly had immense appreciation for Minnie. There ought to be an award for any girl who can fully take a shaft inside each of her passages, much less just one from behind as Alice was doing now.

The Hatter just stayed there, keeping her fully stuffed, as he leaned over and placed kisses on her back. Alice clenched around him, feeling his thickness penetrating her.

She closed her eyes. Taking in the moment. She could feel the Hatter's hands on her shoulders again, kneading out the stiffness there. She could hear Minnie and the Hare kissing each other again. She could smell the lust wafting up from their bodies' cores. She kissed Minnie's back and could taste the salty sweat upon her.

"You are so lovely," the Hatter said.

Alice pushed her hips forward. Enough to ease a bit of the Hatter's cock out of her and then slowly pushed back against him. The re-entrance was just as fiery as when he first inched that thick cock into her, and just as smooth, thanks to Minnie's tongue.

Alice repeated the small movement. Back and forth, controlling the in and out strokes of his cock.

Minnie moaned. It was only then that Alice

realized moving her hips forward to ease out the Hatter's cock was pushing the spout deeper into Minnie. Alice started up a slow rhythm, moving forward to push into Minnie, moving back to take more of the Hatter's lovely cock. She moaned with the rush.

Hot! Hot! Hot! His thickness opened Alice wide and Alice rubbed herself with rapid fingertips. The Hare joined the rhythm, thrusting into Minnie as Alice moved out.

"Yes!" Minnie called out. "Faster!"

Alice grabbed hold of Minnie's waist and thrust inside her tea-filled hole. The Hatter followed suit. Alice felt the Hatter's hands on her waist and thrust his full length into her, pushing her deeper into Minnie.

"That's it!" Minnie shouted. "Yes!"

Alice felt the constant shuttling of the Hatter's huge cock. The blissful heat set Alice ablaze. She went back to rubbing her clit as the Hatter did the work, thrusting into Alice, pushing her into Minnie. His strokes pushed into both the women, and they moved together, jolted together, cried out together. Alice felt connected to Minnie, like twins experiencing the same feelings. She slid her free hand down Minnie's arm, finding Minnie's hand and clasped tight. Together they held hands as the Hatter thrust into them, pushed into them, filling them. The Hare kissed Minnie deeply. Alice understood the loving desire the Hare had for Minnie because Alice, too, wanted to make sure Minnie felt the loving orgasm she so deserved. Alice felt a throbbing behind her. The Hatter was close. And that was all due to me, Alice recognized. Lovely Alice. The Hatter feels this way because of me.

"Oh!" cried Minnie. "I think I'm going to explode!"

"Me too!" the Hare said.

"Yes!" Alice smiled. "That's an orgasm! Let it happen!"

Minnie cried out and the Hare cried out at the same time.

Alice saw their beautiful bodies tense, shake, and shudder, and she rammed three fingers deep inside herself.

She felt her walls pulse around her fingers. She squeezed her eyes shut. She cried out. Her muscles tensed. She clenched around the Hatter's cock. All her nerves erupted. Visions of fire sparks bursting. The Hatter thrust and pinned his waist against hers and Alice felt his seed fill deep within her uncharted passage.

And Alice realized she was wrong. Orgasms do come in different colors.

She opened her eyes, head spinning, and dizzy. And soon she felt the table at her knees, the cool air blowing against her legs and face, and the heat of Minnie at her chest and the Hatter's cock softening within her.

The four of them stayed still, all of them connected. All of them one. Alice's legs felt wobbly. She had to rest on Minnie's back. The Hatter lay on top of Alice. She felt the weight of his love. Made the love feel solid. Real.

"Okay," Minnie said. "I'm getting squished."

The Hatter climbed off the table, and Alice carefully pulled out of Minnie, backing up on the table.

The Hatter caressed Alice's face and said, "Lovely. Thank you."

Alice smiled and kissed his cheek.

She saw Minnie and the Hare holding each other. The Hatter went to their side. When they saw him, they each reached out an arm to him. The Hatter put his head close to theirs to hug them as best as he could.

Alice thought, *I believe I actually had an orgasm. Maybe that was all it took, to be penetrated in that untouched passage.*

Alice took the spout in her hands and said, "This is like a regular, ceramic teapot."

She felt her waist tingle and the teapot separated itself from her.

She set it on the table, climbed off, and put her underwear back on.

It was time to move on. Alice turned to wish her friends good-bye, but she saw that Minnie had turned herself around, lying with her back on the Hare and now had the Hatter on top of her in her arms. They were in a sweet embrace, in their own world. Alice decided not to disturb them and wandered towards the forest.

Wow, Alice thought. *I actually had an orgasm.*

She realized the truth. Since she could climax, she wasn't a freak after all. She could, in fact, love a man as much as any other girl. And just wait until Carol hears about her successful orgasm!

Alice giggled. "I feel like I'm walking on air!" Her giggles turned to laughter as she floated just above the ground, the earth no longer pinching her feet. Alice scampered into the forest of plants letting the puffs of air at her feet lead the way.

Chapter 18

SEVERAL minutes into the forest, Alice had thought it best to return to earth and had recited a simile to get herself walking normally on the ground again. She came to a tree with a knob sticking out of it, at about waist level. The knob looked very much like a doorknob, shaped and carved by a carpenter. It drew her.

The doorknob's surface was cool and smooth. Of course it was ridiculous to think it would actually turn, as if to open but if she wanted to get home, she knew it was best to try everything.

Click.

Alice couldn't believe it. The doorknob turned. When she tugged on it, an embedded door swung open.

Curiosity ever strong, she peered in. Wooden stairs led down to a lit room below. She descended the stairway, steps creaking each time she put her barefoot on the smooth cool wood.

At the bottom of the stairs, Alice found herself back in the hallway of doors. They looked like the same ones she'd seen from when she'd fallen down the well. Now that she was so small, all the doors were much too big for her.

All but one.

Wait! The hanged man! Her heart pounded at the prospect of seeing the hanged man again. Her eyes darted all around but there was no sign of him. She found the tiny door by the coffee table. From her time with the caterpillar, she still had the pieces of mushroom in her pockets. She had what she needed.

Alice chewed on some mushroom to make herself stretch tall enough to pick up the small key from the table. Once she had the key in her long fingers, she nibbled on the other piece of mushroom. The tiny door got bigger. She nibbled a bit more. The door rose to meet her. She had shrunk down back to her tiny size and could now fit through the door.

The key fit perfectly. Alice rushed through, and found herself outdoors surrounded by red and white roses. A bright sun shone upon her in a blue sky. Normal-sized roses? A blue sky? Did she make it home? She had managed to have an orgasm, after all.

And Caterpillar showed her what to do with a cock if one were in front of her face. She had the sexual discovery she needed. Maybe now she was home. The heady fragrance of roses made her sigh at the promise. With the excitement of possibly making it home, her gaze darted across the roses around her to see if she recognized them.

Her heart sank. This was not her family's garden. Was she still stuck in the strange world?

Her bare feet traced a footpath of smooth gravel all the way to the main road. The gravel crunched beneath her feet without hurting her soles.

Alice came upon a strange man licking the roses at the side of the road. The man was flat. Literally, two-dimensional. The trunk of his body was squashed and flat like a piece of paper. His flat body was dressed in green overalls with three red hearts on his breast pocket.

But his head and limbs were normal.

The man stood over one of the rose bushes. He guided one of the white roses to his lips, and licked its petals.

At least, it was a white rose.

Or was it red?

Actually, it looked like red liquid dripped from his tongue as he painted the white petals red.

"Are you bleeding?" Alice asked.

The man jumped. "You—you scared me."

"I'm sorry, it's just—your mouth is all red. Are

you bleeding?"

"No, I'm painting." He glanced over his shoulder down the road as if to see if anyone was coming. "I'm the gardener, and was supposed to plant red roses for the queen." He rushed his words in a conspiratorial tone. "There was a mix-up with the seeds. Some white roses grew with the red roses. If I don't paint these white roses red before the queen arrives, she'll have my head!" He rushed both hands over his crotch to emphasize his point, and then guided the white rose he was painting back to his lips.

Alice stifled a laugh. What was the queen going to do with his flat body, cut a hole where his penis should be?

"I know a gardener who works in my yard. His name is Jack." Alice wasn't really sure why she said this. Maybe it was because she didn't know what else to say.

A distant voice boomed. "Here comes the queen!"

Alice and the gardener turned toward the road. A parade of flat people marched in front of a high seat being carried by more flat people. On the high seat sat a woman who must have been the queen.

"No! No! No!" The gardener said in a panicked voice. "I'm not finished! If she sees what I've done she'll have my head!"

Alice didn't think he had anything to worry about. Surely the queen would understand a mix-up with the red rose and white rose seeds. But what if the queen were as ruthless as people had been saying?

"Quick," Alice said. "Hide under my dress!"

"Thank you! Thank you!" The gardener folded over and positioned himself between Alice's legs.

The processional of flat people approached. They wore military uniforms. When they were close enough, Alice could see the rows of hearts like medals across their coats. These flat soldiers kept their heads at attention, staring straight down the road while passing Alice as if she wasn't there.

At the same moment the raised platform with the queen was passing Alice, Alice was about to breathe a sigh of relief when the queen shouted, "Stop!"

Alice stood tall and demure as was expected before a queen. Though she'd never actually met one.

The entire processional came to a halt. The queen gazed down her nose at Alice. A beautiful woman with challenging eyes. Long, black hair under a golden crown, and red lips in the shape of a heart. "Who is that woman?" the queen yelled at a soldier.

"Not known, your highness!" the soldier called out.

"Idiot," the queen muttered. To Alice she said, "Who are you?"

"I'm Alice." She tried her best to curtsey without hitting the gardener beneath her.

"Well, Alice, why are these roses white?"

Alice felt a finger pull aside her underwear, exposing her pussy to the open air.

"How should I know?" Alice gulped, and suppressed a shiver.

The queen grit her teeth. "Where is the gardener?"

Alice felt the gardener's warm breath against her exposed cleft. A tongue stroked along the side of her folds. Even though no one could see her pussy being licked by the gardener, having them all watch her getting turned on was enough to make her blush.

"The gardener?" Alice asked giving way to the embarrassment she felt by smiling.

"Yes. Where is the gardener?"

His moist tongue ran across the other side of her folds. Alice felt herself open up. What was he doing? Painting her pink folds red? Did he think she had a rose between her legs? The gardener found her deep opening. Alice felt his hot tongue slip deeper, painting her with fervent strokes.

"The...gardener?" Alice managed.

The queen huffed and exasperated breath. "Do you even know what a gardener is?"

Yes, Alice thought. *I'm getting to know his tongue very well.*

He discovered her nub and licked around it, in the most luscious way, taking his time to make luxurious circles. Alice quivered.

"Yes." Alice sighed. That was the spot. Her juices dripped down to her knees.

"Well then." The queen over-enunciated her

words. "Since you know what a gardener is. Then maybe. You can tell me. If you've seen. The gardener."

Round and round her clit with hot, slick licks, the gardener painted Alice.

"The gardener?" Alice moaned.

She couldn't believe she had an entire unsuspecting audience watch her as she was being tasted, and turned on in a most delightful way.

"Oh, for heaven's sake! Do you or do you not know where the gardener is?!"

His tongue moved away from her nub and pushed his so clever tongue inside of her. Her whole body flushed as he slipped into her, caressing all around her inner walls.

"Oh!" Alice cried, her body trembling. *Never in all her years...* the thought faded as her body heated.

"You're a strange bird," the queen said. "But your face has good color."

The queen turned to a soldier beside her. "Invite her to my croquet game."

Alice's body flushed hot. The gardener kept up his tongue twirling. She worked hard to stay still. She wanted to pump on his tongue. She wanted him to put a warm smart finger inside her ass. She was close to climax. A well-placed finger would get her there for sure. She wanted to squirm. She wanted more and she knew what she wanted. Heat pulsed through her and she held herself still.

The soldier spoke. She heard him through her heat.

"You, Alice, are hereby invited to join the queen in a game of croquet. Please follow us."

The processional marched past her. Alice didn't want to move, not yet.

Alice felt the tongue slip out, and a finger reposition her underwear. She sighed. The gardener came out from under her dress.

"Thank you for saving me," he said. "I am truly grateful. Oh, and I painted your rose red."

"I know." She took a deep breath and blew out to relieve some of the tension.

"Are you alright, Alice?"

Alice giggled at the way he didn't seem to realize how she'd felt his every lick.

"You better join the processional to the queen's croquet game, now. Goodbye!" And off went the flat gardener with his talented tongue.

Alice sighed again.

It was time to find a way back home. Who else but the queen would have the power to help Alice return home? Alice decided she should befriend the queen, and if that meant playing croquet with her, so be it.

Playing croquet with a queen! Alice relished the thought. *My friends will be so jealous when they find out!*

Chapter 19

ALICE watched as all the soldiers of the processional had passed. Then came the villagers from the start of her adventure, those ridiculous naked men from the campfire and led by their elder. She joined behind them, hoping she wouldn't be recognized as the woman who killed one of their men. One of them bumped into her.

She turned to whoever it was. "Pardon me."

It was Rabbit. His eyes widened. "You!"

Alice raised her hands in innocence. "I swear it was an accident. I didn't mean for any harm to come to him."

" 'Any harm?' " Rabbit looked appalled. " 'Any harm?!' You talk as if he experienced a hazard of some sort. You killed him! Are you saying his death was an unfortunate mishap? A bad day? Rotten luck? One too many black cats crossed his path? Walked under too many ladders, did he? His death was just one of his unpleasant memories? Didn't throw enough salt over his shoulder? Is that it?"

"No! Of course not!" Alice's gut clamped tight. "I feel awful about it."

Rabbit looked at Alice. She could feel her eyes stinging. All at once it hit her. The denial. Her denial. She spent all this time running away, never acknowledging that man's death.

What did that say about her as a human being? Didn't she realize how his friends could never see him again? Talk to him again? Enjoy his company? She shook her head to voice her heart-felt apology, but instead Rabbit startled her with his next words.

"Aw, don't worry about it. He came back to life."

"What?" She wiped away the wetness of her eyes.

"One of the villagers got careless. He knows the taboo against reciting clichés, similes, and metaphors. But when he looked at the smile on the dead man's face, he said, 'It's like he's still alive.' So the dead man came back to life."

Alice couldn't believe it. "Wow! That's great, right? Where is he now?"

"In his cottage. After he came back to life, he found some slippery jelly, locked himself in his cottage, and we haven't seen him since."

Slippery jelly? "But he's okay? He's still alive?"

"He's fine. He seems to be making a lot of discoveries."

"Why do you say that?"

"Because everyone can hear him from inside his cottage saying, 'Oh, yes! Oh, yes! Oh, yes!' "

Alice had the instant image of the man sliding a well-lubed hand up and down his cock. She smiled and bit on the tip of her finger to keep herself from revealing what she knew. But what mattered was that he was alive. The weight of her guilt lifted. She felt light, as if everything would be okay. Now she could go to the croquet game and fully enjoy herself like all the other players until she could find a way to get home.

Wait a second, Alice thought. *Isn't the duke supposed to be at the game, too?*

Alice swiveled to see if the duke was in the processional. She didn't see him.

"Where's the duke?" Alice asked Rabbit.

"The queen sentenced him to have his head chopped off," Rabbit said.

"You mean," Alice said, "the tip of his..." She burst out laughing and covered her mouth. The duke was going to have the top of his penis cut off! She was a little sorry for the duke's pain. But not really.

"It's not funny!" Rabbit said.

"I know, I know" Alice tried to stifle her laugh, but soon it exploded out from her mouth in loud barks. She grabbed her middle, the laughing hurt so much, in such a good way.

Rabbit must think her the most cold-blooded person alive.

She tried to control herself, breathing in, then out, waving her hands at her face.

Rabbit looked appalled, again.

"I'm sorry." Alice couldn't stop her grinning. "I'm sorry, I'm sorry." Deep breaths, she told herself.

In.

Out.

In.

Out.

Alice finally said, "So how come the queen is having them cut off his—" She exploded in laughter again. She had to stop walking. Rabbit stopped beside her. The villagers around her moved past them. Alice doubled over, letting loose howls of laughter, clutching her side again. After the guffaws were out, and the chuckles and the giggles, she breathed and felt finally she had control of herself.

She stood upright. She felt dizzy.

"Are you quite done?" Rabbit asked sternly.

"Yes." Alice breathed deeply. "I think so."

She wondered when was the last time she laughed this much. She couldn't remember. It felt great. Almost as great as an orgasm.

She asked, "Why did the queen sentence him?"

"He was late to the croquet game," Rabbit said.

"The queen doesn't tolerate tardiness."

"So, this croquet game we're going to wasn't the one that he was invited to?"

"No, no," Rabbit said. "He was invited to the post-early-afternoon game. There have been three more since then."

"Three?"

"Yes, the pre-mid-afternoon game, the mid-afternoon game, and the post-mid-afternoon game."

"And which one are we attending?"

"The pre-late-afternoon game."

Alice cracked a smile and clamped down on the giggles that threatened to erupt.

She was walking with Rabbit now as they approached a wide expanse of green. The entire processional had arrived at an enormous grassy field enclosed by red rose bushes.

They heard an announcement, "Places everyone!"

The flat soldiers ran to their places, bending over into arches.

"What queer arches," Alice said. She looked around to see where the balls were. She saw a spot by the bushes where dozens of crabs were slowly stepping and stumbling over each other. These crabs had spherical shells, instead of the flat shells that Alice had always seen at the seaside. Their legs were just long enough to shift across the ground. Otherwise, it looked like they could roll head over tail quite easily.

"What queer balls," Alice said. She looked on the

ground for mallets, but didn't see any.

"Where are the mallets?" Alice asked Rabbit.

"There." Rabbit pointed to a row of shirtless men. Some buff, some lean, some plump, some broad-shouldered. And *mmm*, Alice liked the chiseled chin on one of the broad-shouldered, bare-chested men. His chest was particularly buff and tan, as if he spent many hours in the sun working his body in honest labor.

"Mallets," the queen shouted, "Prepare yourselves!"

The men took off their pants and Alice's jaw dropped. Their penises were all incredibly long. They were so long they practically reached to the ground. Like a third leg. They weren't even hard, yet! Alice looked at all the dangling cocks. Her pussy tingled.

What would it be like to have one of those stuffed inside of her?!

Lord, she was getting wet just at the thought of it. What would it be like to have that gorgeous chiseled-chin man on top of her, guiding his length into her, inch after inch, until he held her in his arms, and had her fully stretched with his cock? And what would his thrusts feel like? Each stroke would take a delicious forever, wouldn't it?

Alice felt her entire body heat up all over, her nipples hardened. Her breathing came short.

"Well?" Rabbit said.

"Nothing!" Alice put a hand to her mouth as if it

would cover her thoughts.

"What?"

"What?" Alice felt like she was caught with her hand fisting the cookie jar.

Rabbit looked confused. "I was just asking if you were going to pick your mallet," he said. "Everyone else has."

Sure enough, all the other players were walking beside one of the naked men. She was in luck. No one had picked her chiseled-chin man with the very buff chest.

Alice walked up to him, smiled, and took his hand. He smiled back. He even had the cutest dimples.

She heard someone laugh and mutter, "She picked a narrow one." Alice examined the man's hanging glory. She supposed it *was* narrower than the others, but didn't see the big deal. It was still close to dragging along the ground.

"What's your name?" She asked her mallet.

"Charlie." He smiled again and showed off his matching dimples.

"I'm Alice," she said. Then wondered what else to say. "You have a very lovely...mallet." *Stupid, Alice! Stupid! Stupid!*

"Thank you." He blushed.

How cute! She felt herself falling into his brown eyes, his smile, those dimples...

"Players, find your places!" a voice announced.

There was no time to gaze further into his eyes and continue her fantasy, since all the other players were leading their mallets on the field.

She led Charlie to her ball on the field, surrounded by cards bent as arches. She glanced around quickly but didn't see Rabbit or the queen.

Her marked ball – a crab with a single stripe upon its shell – sat motionless, ready to be tapped. Now how was she supposed to do this? She huddled behind Charlie, wrapped her arms around his waist, and put everything she could into lifting his entire body. She managed somehow to lift him by leaning far back and swinging him and his long cock in the general direction of the crab. His cock swung along with his body, but since it wasn't any longer than his legs, it swung much too high to get anywhere near the crab.

Alice felt Charlie's stomach tighten under her hands.

"That tickles," Charlie said.

She dropped him, putting his feet back on the ground. *Boy, he's heavy!* She watched to see how the others were doing it. She noticed they had their men-mallets bend over onto their hands and feet making an upside-down V with their bodies. From their hips, the point on the V, hung their cocks close enough to the ground to swing at the crabs. The other players swung the cocks to hit the crab balls.

Alice thought it was silly, and maybe a little sexy,

especially if she was going to touch Charlie's cock.

She guided Charlie to bend over. His knees were straight, his hands on the grass. His dick swung free. She adjusted his body close enough to the crab, and positioned herself behind him, bent over him. She wrapped her arms around him to get both hands on his length. Heat surged between her legs, making her feel a little giddy. She paused.

Would she ever get her hands on a cock this long again? She felt its heat, its softness in her hands. She stroked his dick.

"Hey, that tickles," Charlie said in a sweet voice. Alice stopped stroking.

Time to play croquet. She lifted his dick back, and swung it against her ball. No good. His soft cock just dragged over the crab.

Alice looked around again to see how the others did it. They stroked the cock first to get it hard, then they swung it against their ball. Her instincts had been correct.

She noticed their rhythm. Stroke, stroke, stroke, swing. Stroke, stroke, stroke, swing.

Alice grabbed hold of his cock again and stroked it. She slid her hands down and up, down and up. She felt like she was running her hands along a warm rope. But it wasn't doing much. His cock just wasn't getting stiff enough to function as a mallet.

She thought for a moment. Aha!

"My hands are like vibrating pads," Alice said.

That did it! Alice's fingers webbed together and her hands buzzed. As she guided her now transformed hands along the underside of Charlie's shaft, Charlie moaned. His cock hardened into a fine staff. She felt her heart quicken.

Now to swing it.

"My hands are just like they normally are," Alice said.

Her fingers separated. She grabbed hold of Charlie, ready to swing. But the ball had walked several inches away.

Alice repositioned Charlie to the ball. Standing behind him, she bent over his butt and back, pressed herself against him to reach his cock again. She quickly set out to pump him to his full length. With her hands back on his hard, hot tool, it didn't take much to get him back to full length. He didn't need vibrating pads now.

Charlie moaned louder. "It's never felt this good before."

"Yeah?" Alice said. "You like that?"

"Oh, yes!"

So do I, she thought.

Alice wondered if this was her mission. Her calling. To help others who had never before experienced an orgasm. Alice squeezed herself closer to his body, pressing her breasts into his back, her nipples as hard as marbles. Her hands shuttled back and forth on his lovely cock. Charlie gasped, held his breath before exhaling and gasped again. She rubbed faster, his dick so long, so hard, so good.

She could feel herself getting wet. With her head resting against his back, she could hear the pounding of his heart. She warmed more between her legs.

This was her doing. She was causing him to grow so big, his heart to beat this rapidly, his breaths to become uneven. But was she really attractive enough to make men feel this way? Or could any pair of hands have this effect? After all, Charlie wasn't even looking at her face. Though the sounds he made sure were having an effect on her!

"Alice," he cried. "What are you doing to me?"

His body shook. And oh, how Alice's panties felt soaked. She rubbed her chest up and down his back, her waist thrusting into his. She felt his cock throbbing in her hands. He was close. Up and down that full length, as fast as she could go. Knowing she was giving Charlie a pleasure he had never before known made her feel so hot. She pushed her hips into him, rubbing her nipples on his back. Why did she feel like she might be able to orgasm from this?

"Yes!" Charlie cried. Ropes of white seed shot into the grass. She twisted her hands as she stroked him, wringing out his cock intent on getting all his cum out of him, wanting him to feel the full extent of his pleasure.

His whole body tightened, tensed up, shuddered, and shook. With spurt after spurt, Charlie cried out his pleasure. Alice pulsed hot deep within herself. Holding hard onto his cock, she saw the stripes of white she painted along the grass, proof of her power over his ecstasy.

But not proof enough. Time to test what her face could do.

Alice guided him to stand upright. She squatted in front of his long, dangling mallet and gazed up at him with a smile. He smiled back. Lord, those dimples!

In one hand, she held the tip up and out so his length came straight out from his body. It hung from his waist to her hand like a thick jump rope. With her other hand, she ran a finger along the underside, following the path she imagined his seed took. From the base, her finger started that long journey, drawing the path.

She watched his face.

His eyes closed.

Her finger passed the middle of his length.

His mouth fell open.

She drew towards the tip.

His breaths quickened.

Alice's own breaths become uneven. The tip rewarded her journey with a final drop of white. She dabbed it onto her finger and made sure he was looking at her face as she brought the salty drop to her lips.

He gave a moan that confirmed it! Alice had a face that could make men moan. She was attractive enough…at least to Charlie.

That would have to be good enough, for now.

She let his cock fall and stood up to kiss him. His lips were sweet. She brought his hands to her breasts, showing him to press circles onto them. He rubbed her nipples with his palms. It was Alice's turn to moan.

"So!" A voice startled Alice.

She spun around. It was the Cheshire cat in a tree. Alice realized where she was. Several croquet players were staring at her. Her ears got hot. Her neck itched. Alice laughed.

How could she have completely forgotten she was at a croquet game? She put her hands over face. How embarrassing!

"So!" the cat said again. "How are you getting off?"

As she turned back to the cat, she felt some relief that the other players returned to their game. She scowled. "Don't you mean 'how am I getting on'?"

"That too." The cat smiled its toothy smile.

"I'm afraid I'm not doing very well," Alice said. "I haven't been able to hit the ball once."

"Not what you're used to?"

"Not at all."

"And how do you like the mallets?" The cat's smile had a mischievous flavor to it.

Alice saw right through his game, but had an idea. She whispered to the cat in a husky voice, "I just love the mallets. Holding that hot, long rod in my hands. Stroking that cock good and hard. Rubbing it from root to tip, watching the man's face tighten with delight. His legs go weak."

The cat grinned wider.

"I never thought they could be so long. And just imagining that thing inside of me. Oh my Lord!" Alice closed her eyes and held herself as if she were picturing the erotic scene. "But you know what I like even more than the mallets?"

"Tell me!"

"The croquet balls," Alice said. "They're the cat's pajamas!"

Flannel pajamas appeared on the back half of the Cheshire cat's body. Crab legs stuck out from the side of the pajamas, their claws snapping blindly at the air.

The cat's expression changed into a tired look of exasperation. "Ha." He paused. "Ha."

Alice laughed at how ridiculous he looked. "So much for your hindsight."

"No, no," the cat said. "I had some memory of the pajama moment."

"So why did you let me say it?"

"Because I also have the memory of using it as a reason to say how it looks like your dream of having a mallet inside you is coming true."

Strong arms embraced Alice from behind.

"You feel so good, Alice." She felt Charlie's voice of desire at her ear. He leaned her over. She heard her skirt rustling as Charlie lifted the hem behind her.

"Let me show you what you did to me," he whispered.

She got hot with anticipation. *This is it. The moment I lose my virginity.* There was something sad about not losing it to Jack. But he had his chance.

Her underwear was whisked down. She felt him guide his tip past her entrance.

She sighed with delight.

Considering what playing with Charlie's mallet did to her, that cock was just what she needed.

He pushed in further, a gentle never-ending push. She was so wet for him, it hardly mattered how quickly he entered her. In. And in. Lord, he was so big! He reached the depth of her.

"Like a snake!" She cried. "It's like a snake!" Charlie's length coiled inside her, allowing more of him to enter. Alice felt his hands knead her nipples as he continued filling her, opening her. In. And in. Charlie pushed until finally, Alice felt his waist connect with hers. She was full of Charlie.

She gasped at the sensation of this hot, massive cock coiled inside of her. But something was missing. Wasn't a cock this big supposed to get her to climax? Or did she really need one in her rear to get there? Alice decided to try something daring.

"It feels as hard and stiff as it was before," Alice breathed.

Alice cried out as Charlie's cock stretched her

more. It tried to unwind itself inside of her and fought to push open her walls. Charlie sucked in his breath through clenched teeth. It must have been incredibly uncomfortable having a hard cock twisted so.

The queen's voice shouted in the distance, "The tarts! Someone stole the tarts!"

Alice and Charlie stilled, and glanced in the queen's direction. She seemed to be glaring straight at them. Her majesty stepped at a good clip towards them.

"You better stop," Alice sighed to Charlie. Charlie grit his teeth and began to pull out. Alice held her breath, and pressed Charlie's hands against her breasts, making sure he didn't put his hands down just yet. Lord, the length of that thing. He pulled out. And out. It stretched her folds, feeling hard between them. It felt so good. She didn't really want to stop.

Alice found she could no longer keep his hands on her chest, not if he needed to pull completely out of her. Charlie stepped back from Alice. She stepped forward. Out. And out.

Why didn't that do it for her? Alice wondered. Why did she feel closer to orgasm handling Charlie's mallet in her hands than having it inside her? It didn't make sense.

The queen was closer, just a few yards away. Charlie's last few inches slipped out of Alice. Alice adjusted her dress to cover her legs.

"Who is that?!" the queen demanded, pointing

behind Alice. Alice followed the line of her finger to the Cheshire cat who was still grinning at the show he just watched.

"That's a Cheshire cat," Alice said.

"I hate this part," the cat said.

"Well," the queen said. "Wipe that smile off his face!"

Alice suddenly found she had no control. Her hand brushed across the cat's face. His smile drifted completely off his whiskers and floated away.

The cat grabbed his smile with a paw and placed it back on his face. Only it was less of a smile and more of a grin-and-bear-it look.

The queen said, "He looks suspicious!"

"I best be going, now," the cat said and vanished.

"Where did he go?" The queen said to no one in particular. Then she turned to Alice. "Where did he go?"

"How should I know?" Alice said. "He's not my cat."

"Then whose cat is he?"

"He belongs to the duke," Alice said.

"Fetch the duke!" the queen shouted. "And find out who stole my tarts!"

The flat soldiers stepped out of their positions as arches and scrambled off to heed the queen's commands.

"As usual," the queen said, "no winner in croquet. Everyone must return for the post-late-afternoon game!" The queen scuttled away.

Alice stepped close to Charlie, putting her hands on his chest as she looked up into his eyes. "I suppose I should bring you back to the other mallets." Her pussy clenched and she growled as she gave his cock one last squeeze. So hard to let go.

She kissed his cheek and took him by the hand, leading him to the row of naked men, their cocks dangling close to the ground. Only Charlie's glistened in the afternoon sun.

Chapter 20

A LICE walked back towards the area where the other players stood. Suddenly an oozing arm wrapped around her waist, a stench violating her nose.

"Time to deal with you." Bad breath smacked her face.

Alice paled. It was the duke.

"I have to thank you," he said with malice, "for getting me out of prison. Now I can't wait to shove my cock so deep into you, your eyes will be bleeding."

Alice's body tensed for a fight. Her gut churned heavy.

"Do you know why I don't take you right here?" he said. "It's because the queen is near. Now, where shall we complete our unfinished business?"

She could turn him into a mouse as the Cheshire

cat suggested, but was that too cruel? Think! Alice told herself. Think! What could she do? How could she escape?

"Ahem!" the queen interrupted their conversation. Never had Alice thought she'd be so relieved to see the queen. Could she convince the queen to send the duke back to prison for his head to be chopped off? Alice wasn't sure she could convince the queen of anything. No. The best solution for the moment was to get the duke to go away.

"I know just the place," Alice whispered quickly to the duke. "Meet me at that shed over there," she pointed with her eyes, "sneak in and I'll be there soon."

The queen said at the duke, "Either you or your head must be off! Which will it be?"

"A pl-pl-pleasure to see you, your m-m-majesty," and off the duke ran.

"Now." The queen turned to Alice. "Are you coming to the trial or not?"

"Trial?"

"Yes. We've found the thief who stole the tarts. Come along!"

Alice followed the queen. As she quickened her pace to keep up, she thought about the strange way the queen governed this wonderland. The restrictions against clichés, similes and metaphors were understandable. Alice witnessed firsthand the dangers of and the power of words. But why cut off all the tips of men's penises?

"Your majesty," Alice started.

"What is it?" the queen said.

"Why do you…that is, I've noticed how you tend to…what I mean is—"

"Spit it out, woman!"

"How come so many men are having their…heads cut off?"

The queen took in a deep breath, sighed, and then stopped walking. Alice watched the queen open her mouth to say something, and stop herself. The queen did this several times, gazing at the sky, searching, opening her mouth to say something, and then shutting her mouth, apparently changing her mind.

"When I was a princess," the queen said at last, "I looked forward to the day I would meet my prince. I pictured our courtship. Would he take me to dance in ballrooms? Would he sing to me in a bower? Would he take me upon his stallion to a secluded beautiful place in the forest?"

For the first time Alice saw the queen smile with the sweetness of love.

"I used to take walks along these fields, practicing my likes."

"Your likes?" Alice asked.

"Yes, 'the clouds above me are like cotton candy,' 'the wind is like an ocean breeze,' that kind of 'like'."

Alice stared at the pink puffs in the sky. She

breathed deep and tasted the fresh, salty air.

"All the while, I was wondering who my prince would be and how we would spend our time together."

The queen's eyes drifted to the ground. She frowned.

"I was saving myself—" The queen stopped. She gave Alice a troubled expression. "I had a special rose. I was planning to give it to my prince."

Alice nodded. She understood the queen's meaning.

"And it was taken," the queen said quietly. "Against my will." She whispered with anger.

Alice said nothing. She didn't know what to say.

"I know it's ridiculous." The queen pursed her lips. "To surround myself with red roses as if somehow, that would bring back my own. Bring back a prince. But still, I let my foolishness of having all these flowers…"

The queen let the silence linger.

"Who took it?" Alice asked.

"I don't know. I…my back was turned. All I remember was his foul breath. Like chili pepper."

Alice gasped.

"Come now," the queen said in an imperious tone, intimate girl talk seemingly forgotten. "The trial is about to begin."

Chapter 21

ALICE followed the queen across the grassy field to a courtroom laid out on the green grass. There were two rows of chairs for the jury, a seating arrangement for onlookers, and there sat the queen in her throne across from the suspect. The suspect was a flat man with a hood over his head. His normal-looking hands and feet were wrapped in chains spiked to the ground.

"Delicious!" A voice said by way of greeting. Among the arriving onlookers, Alice saw it was Caterpillar! He wore a big, welcoming smile.

"I don't understand," Alice said. "Last I saw you, you were becoming a cocoon. But you look the same as before."

"I was in that cocoon to realize my full potential. Inside I had time to think. If I wanted to get to the best I could be, I needed to first know where I was starting from. The more I dwelled on who I already was, the more I realized how I didn't want to be any different. I am Caterpillar. Smoking gun and all."

Alice ran into his arms to give him the hug he so deserved, and took comfort in feeling all of his hands enfold her. Caterpillar's words and confidence warmed her chest. She wondered if it would do her well to follow his example.

"Come to order!" the queen announced.

It was time to sit down. Alice bid Caterpillar a quiet farewell. She looked for a place to sit, but all of the onlookers' seats were taken. Alice saw Rabbit in one of the seats. Without asking, she sat on his lap. He frowned, but said nothing and didn't move her off his lap.

"Jury," the queen said, "what is your verdict?"

"Uh, not yet, your majesty," said a courtroom orderly standing beside the queen. "First we must hear the evidence against the Jack of Hearts."

"Oh, very well." The queen waved her hand as if to say move along. "Go on."

The orderly announced, "Bring in the first witness!"

Two flat soldiers, the Eight of Hearts and the Nine of Hearts, escorted the elder of the village in. Rabbit whispered to Alice. "This isn't very comfortable." He patted her hips.

She reflected on how she could orgasm with the Hatter's cock in her ass, but Charlie's mallet didn't get her there. Was she really only able to come with a prick up her rear? Alice had an idea. "You wanted to know what a pussy feels like?" She grinned at Rabbit.

"Yes?"

"Well, I'll show you something that feels better than that!"

Alice discreetly lifted her dress, pulled her panties down, and sat on Rabbit, skin on skin.

The queen asked the elder, "What's your testimony?"

"I saw the Jack in Rabbit's cottage," the old man said. "And it wasn't even his cottage. It was Rabbit's."

Alice reached behind her and rubbed Rabbit's cock. She had to see. Had to know for sure if this was the only way she could climax. His length hardened hot in her hand.

The queen said, "Jury, what's your verdict?"

"Um," the orderly said, "there is more evidence to view, your Majesty."

"Yes, yes," the queen said. "Call the next witness."

"Bring in the next witness!" shouted the orderly.

The soldiers escorted the elder out and brought in Caterpillar.

Alice brought Rabbit's tip to her ass. "It's as moist as a tongue," she said. His length became slippery and the head slid right in.

Alice sucked in her breath. She clenched around him and felt him stretch her entrance.

"Alright, Caterpillar," the queen said. "Present your evidence."

"I was sitting on my mushroom at the time the tarts were stolen," he said.

"So?" the queen said.

"So the thief clearly was not me. And since the Jack of Hearts is also not me, the thief must be the Jack."

"Yes!" the queen said. "That proof is solid."

Alice ignored the ridiculous testimonies of the witnesses. She was just glad to know Caterpillar found his true self. Now to find her own. She focused on relaxing, letting herself inch down on Rabbit's cock, getting closer and closer to becoming fully seated in his lap. Rabbit groaned. Alice reached all the way down, her rim clenching, pulsing, throbbing around his hot shaft. And yet, something still wasn't as good as when the Hatter did it to her. What was missing?

The trial continued its meaningless course, as Alice tried to increase her arousal by moving up and down Rabbit. She felt his cock pushing into her. She lifted herself up, then down, his cock pulling out, pushing in, stretching that narrow secret part of her. But it wasn't enough.

"This isn't working," she whispered to Rabbit.

She sat up, releasing his length completely out of her.

Rabbit wrapped his fist around his cock and worked on himself. "It was! It was!" Alice stood to walk away and waited until the queen was done with her duties. Alice could ask the queen after the trial how to get back home.

The queen said, "What is your verdict?"

The orderly said, "Remove his hood so he can be properly addressed by his jury."

The Eight of Hearts pulled the black cloth from the Jack of Hearts. Alice recognized his face immediately.

She gasped. "No!"

Chapter 22

I T WAS the hanged man, his gorgeous body now hideously flattened. Alice ran to him and lifted his now clean-shaven chin with delicate fingers to peer into his eyes. Without his facial hair, she recognized he was more than just the hanged man. He was Jack. Her Jack. Under his perfect mop of dark and sweaty hair, tired blackness bagged beneath his half-shut eyes. His lips were cracked from dryness, a desperate tongue failing to revive them.

"Hanged man," she whispered.

He awoke at her voice, and seemed to notice his surroundings. With his gaze into her eyes, Alice felt him penetrate her soul.

"Alice." His dry, scratchy voice cracked through his smile. "My big beauty. Ly muv."

He seemed to have forgotten the horrible

accusations around him. All his attention was placed on her. His recognition of who she was, as if nothing else mattered to him except her, made Alice swoon.

"Jack. My dear hanged man." Alice wanted to keep his mind off the trial. "I never had a chance to ask you. How did you know my name?"

"You're the only woman…Your warm love…for my hold cart."

Alice clutched fast to him, holding him as tight as she could.

"Stop that at once!" the queen shouted. "Get that woman away from the Jack!"

Two soldiers clamped their beefy hands on Alice's arms and began dragging her away from the hanged man.

"No!" Alice cried. What could she do? "I know where your tarts are! I know who has them!"

"Wait!" shouted the queen. She looked at Alice with stern eyes. "Where are they?"

"They're in that shed over there," Alice pointed to the nearby wooden hut. "And Queen, the man inside who stole the tarts?" Alice gave the queen a firm look. "He also took your rose."

The queen's mouth opened, and then closed into a thin-lipped grimace. Angry red welts filled her cheeks. The queen stood and stepped down from her throne.

Holding her dress up off the ground, the queen marched towards the shed. "It's like I have fists of steel." Her hands turned to metal and she disappeared into the shed.

In moments, Alice heard the duke cry out.

Alice turned to the Jack of Hearts. It was ludicrous that the Jack was suspected of crimes he could never commit. He only wants to love. And the one he decides to love is his choice. Jack's choice. No matter who he chooses to love, love is never a crime.

She wrapped her arms around him, and held him tight. "Jack, I'm sorry," she said. "I should have known who you really loved, who you really needed. Now I do, Jack. I do."

She held him close. He felt so thin, wasted away in her arms as if she were holding herself.

"Alice."

"I'm sorry," Alice said.

"Alice!"

Alice opened her eyes to a blinding light. Was someone hammering her head? No. It just really hurt. There was someone. In the light.

Alice could make out Jack's face over her. Over her? How did she get to be on the ground?

Jack smiled. "Sleeping beauty awakens!"

"Finally," Carol's voice said. Alice noticed Carol was sitting beside her. Jack was still shirtless wearing only his pants and suspenders.

Alice tried to prop herself up.

"Ow!" She clutched her head to stop it from spinning. "What happened?"

"You fell," Jack said. "Hit your head pretty hard."

"I did? How long was I out?"

"About two minutes."

Alice sat upright.

Ow.

Alice lay back down.

"Take it easy, Alice," Carol said. "If you fall unconscious again, Lois will hate me for not taking better care of you."

Was that wonderland all a dream? Alice struggled at remembering everything that had happened in her dream. *Oh my Lord! I was such a slut!* She felt woozy and the sky was spinning. *I hope I have another dream like that.*

The hum of the family car arriving at the manor sounded in the distance.

"There's Lois with your parents," Carol said. "Are you okay, Alice?"

"I'm fine."

"Good, because I have to go. Alice, I love you, I care about you, and you are the worst study partner ever. I need Lois if I'm ever going to pass my history class." Carol stood up and ran to the car.

Alice and Jack laughed as they watched her go.

"She's an amazing woman, isn't she?" Alice slowly got up off the ground.

"Sure is." Jack helped her stand.

"And funny." She brushed off the dirt from her dress.

"Uh, huh."

"And very pretty, too."

Jack examined Alice's face. "Uh...yeah," he said slowly.

Time to come clean. Alice struggled to find the words. "Jack, I saw how you looked at her, and..."

Jack's quirked a small smile.

"I just want you to know that I think Carol will be a wonderful companion for you."

"Alice," Jack shook his head. "What are you talking about?"

"Face it. She's funnier than me, she's prettier than me,..."

Jack laughed. "If I had a choice between you and Carol, it would be you. Hands down."

Alice gulped.

"The way you get me riled up with all your flirting," Jack smirked. "And seeing you last night..."

Alice blushed.

Jack gave a deep, throaty laugh. "I'll remember that for the rest of my life." His expression turned to a darker place. "But there's no way a gardener could be with someone as upper-class as you. I just can't afford to give you all the things you need."

She felt dizzy. Was that why he never returned her advances? Because he thought he wasn't rich enough?

"You really like me?"

"Are you kidding? I've been admiring you ever

since you made me that celery soup when I was sick three years ago." He smiled. "You said, 'I can't have my favorite gardener in bed all day. There are bushes to trim! Plants to prune! How will I get the chance to interfere with your work if you aren't working?' "

A tear tickled Alice's cheek. Jack used a thumb to wipe it away.

Alice giggled. "It was split-pea."

He gently brushed her hair out of her eyes with his big hand, dirty from gardening. "But I'm not good enough for you."

Alice growled. "Jack, I'm the one decides who I like, no one else."

He nodded. It seemed like he was weighing her words. "You say that, but…" Jack looked as though he were making a decision.

"Jack. I want you and—"

"Good." Jack stepped closer, resting his hands on her waist. His lips were upon hers, her body turning to soup. Of her favorite flavor.

This is real, Alice told herself. *This is true. Not a dream.*

Jack tugged her closer to deepen the kiss. His tongue tasted her lips. His big, firm hand massaged her neck.

Alice pushed away. "Wait," she said. "What about Carol?"

Jack smiled and ran his fingers through her hair. "I don't think Carol will mind."

"But—"

"Follow me," Jack said. He took her hand and led her to the front of the house.

Jack motioned for Alice to crouch down and keep quiet. They crept into the bushes by the front windows. Large, floor-to-ceiling window panels revealed the dining room. They inched closer to the window and peered inside. Alice saw Carol sitting next to Lois at the dining room table, facing out but not seeing Jack and Alice through the window. The way the dining room floor was waist-high to Alice and Jack, they had a clear view of under the table. Lois's hand was exploring between Carol's legs, and Carol's hand lay on Lois's bare leg.

"My sister's a lesbian?!"

Jack smiled.

"How did I not know my sister's a lesbian?" Alice grabbed Jack by the arms. "That is so cool!"

"Come on. Let's go."

"So that's why Lois has been spending all her time with Carol!" Alice whispered.

"Come. Time for me to make you dinner." He grinned. "Back at my place."

Chapter 23

J ACK lived in a small cottage, separate from the servant's quarters. Alice knew that Jack normally ate his meals in the kitchen with the other servants. But tonight was different.

"Sit tight. I'll be right back," he said.

Alice sat alone on his bed and looked around the tiny room. The walls were bare, the floor naked. There was only a bed and a small, plain table and chair. A bedside table with a short candle and candleholder, and a deck of cards.

The sun set. The shadows grew longer and ran their fingers over Alice. She shivered. To pass the time, she turned the cards over to see their faces. It was a tarot deck with colorful illustrations of cups, swords, pentacles, and wands. Alice shuffled through and found what she was looking for. The hanged man. He was naked, except for the loincloth. She turned the card upside down. The face was too small to really tell what sort of face he had.

Alice set the cards down, and watched the door. There was still no sign of Jack. Darkness was beginning to slip in, but she decided to keep the light off.

She looked down at the bed covers and ran her hands along it. The coverlet wasn't as soft as the covers from her own bed. She picked up the pillow. It also wasn't as soft, but she supposed Jack was used to it. She checked the door again. No sound. Alice put the pillow to her face, closed her eyes, and inhaled. She could smell his musky male scent.

The door opened.

Alice threw the pillow to its place on the bed and blurted out, "Nothing!"

"What?" Jack asked.

"What?" Alice asked.

Jack stood still and stared. He looked bemused. He held a pot of food in each hand with a napkin tucked under his arm.

"Will I still be hungry enough for dinner back at the manor?"

"Don't worry," Jack said. "What I brought you won't satisfy your hunger…for food."

Alice laughed, butterflies in her belly.

Jack placed everything on the table and moved the table to Alice so that the bed functioned as her chair. He pulled the one chair over for himself.

Alice admired how his muscles rippled in his arms and chest as he set the table. He caught her admiring him. He smiled. She giggled. Her face felt hot.

Jack pulled matches from his pants pocket, reaching down to that place Alice often dreamed about. He lit the candle. The shadows recoiled to dance on the walls.

Jack picked up the napkin and climbed behind Alice on the bed.

"What are you doing?" Alice laughed.

"Keep your head straight and close your eyes."

Alice did as he asked, and felt the fabric of the napkin blindfold her. Jack's hands rested on her shoulders, massaging them. Alice dropped her head and sighed. He erased the tension in her neck and the worries from her mind.

But he stopped too soon. Then again, Alice guessed anytime a massage ends is too soon. She felt the bed quake and heard Jack climbing off the bed. Alice opened her eyes behind the fabric.

"No peeking," Jack said.

She closed her eyes again. It didn't matter. All she could see with her eyes open was down her nose.

She heard the chair scrape against the floor as though he were moving to sit close to her. The ting of a pot opened.

Silence.

"Open your mouth," Jack said.

"What are you going to do?" Alice laughed again. Her heart sped up in anticipation.

"Trust me," he said.

Silence.

Alice smiled and cautiously opened her mouth. She felt something cold at her lips and touched her tongue to it.

Chocolate!

Dripping from – she gently bit down – a strawberry.

The juices filled her mouth. She shivered, and bit, and chewed.

"Another?" Jack asked softly. His voice rumbled and warmed her belly.

"Yes. Please."

Silence.

"Try this," he said. "And don't bite."

Alice laughed. "Jack!"

"Trust me," he said.

She opened her mouth and tasted a drop of cinnamon pudding on her tongue. She closed her lips. Found her lips wrapped around two of Jack's fingers.

She swirled her tongue around his fingers, licking off the spicy pudding.

Jack groaned.

Alice brought her hands to his and guided his fingers deeper into her mouth.

Jack growled. He removed his fingers. What would come next?

Alice faked a sigh.

"What is it?" he asked.

"I know what I really want," she replied with a sing-song voice, "but I didn't bring my hairbrush."

Suddenly, his lips were planted upon hers. His kiss was urgent, passionate, hungry. When he broke from the kiss, Alice ripped off the blindfold.

She grinned at the pot of strawberries covered in chocolate. "My turn."

"You're going to blindfold me?"

Alice shook her head no.

She picked up one of the strawberries and placed it between her teeth. With a single finger she gave Jack the "come hither" gesture. Jack moved towards Alice like a panther. Her heartbeat quickened.

Jack placed a gentle kiss on her lips, taking the strawberry into his mouth. Alice wrapped her arms around him, sharing with him her lips, her taste, her love.

She completed her kiss and opened her eyes to see him gulping down the strawberry.

"Delicious," he said warmly, his eyes sparkled like diamonds. "Stand up."

Alice did. Jack spun her so her back was to him. He lifted her hair to expose the nape of her neck. With that one gesture, she felt completely naked

Wasn't that strange?

His hands were firm on her shoulders. She could feel his eager breath. Her nipples hardened.

"You're so beautiful," he whispered.

Alice took in a breath and held it, as though fighting to believe his words. She felt a lump lodged in her throat. Jack undid the buttons along the back of her dress. Her spine tingled at the exposure. Jack kissed the nape of her neck, another further down, and further still. She shivered in delight, releasing a moan.

"So beautiful."

Beautiful? Did Jack really think she was beautiful? Or was it just for her to enjoy the moment. Whatever he truly thought, his words had an effect on her. She felt her pussy become wet.

Jack pushed down the sleeves of her dress, slowly lowering her dress down her arms. He placed soft kisses down to the base of her spine. Then he caressed the fabric against her legs as he slid her dress down. It bundled at her ankles.

"Beautiful."

Alice took it in, honoring the tightness in her stomach. Yes, it was still hard to believe him.

But her body still enjoyed every word, every caress. Her breasts ached to be touched, her panties were damp.

His coarse palms swept up her legs, bottom, back, to her shoulders. She felt his warmth, his appreciation for her.

He turned her around so they were face to face. He still had his pants on, and she, her underwear. But it was the way he looked into her eyes that made her feel naked.

Not even her skin protected her from the way he seemed to see straight into her soul.

He seemed to be searching for something within her. Permission, perhaps? No. Something else.

"Do you realize what you do to me?" Jack said, his hands warm on her shoulders.

Alice was startled by the question.

All this time she noticed what he was doing to her...

Jack picked up her hand and placed it on his chest. His heart drummed a tattoo.

"Alice, you are truly a beautiful, beautiful woman."

Feeling the beating of his heart, she was starting to believe his words. Beautiful. She was beautiful. Her eyes welled up as she heard her voice yelling at herself to believe it.

He pulled her into a hug. Her breasts pressed against his bare chest. She fought against the choking sobs. She was not going to ruin the moment. Damn, all these tears coming in spades. She could barely see. Alice breathed through, feeling his body, his love, close to her. His back had so much warm skin for her hands to explore.

She felt desire. A desire to love him. A desire to

show him her gratitude for all his being.

He gently broke their embrace, looked into her eyes, and searching her face he asked, "Are you okay?"

She wanted to be filled with him.

Alice wiped away her tears and nodded. Now it was her turn. She yanked off his suspenders, grabbed the front rim of his pants and said with a hungry voice, "Take this off."

He laughed. "Are you sure?"

"I've been sure of wanting you this way for several years."

She wanted to hold him, to see him for all he truly was. She wanted to show him what she learned from Caterpillar. But that was just a dream. Did her sexual discovery on how to please a man in that wonderland also apply to reality?

He kissed her as he undid his trousers. Alice poured her fingers inside to feel his length, hot in her hands. The first time she felt a real one.

His cock actually pulsed in her hand, hardened. How did something so soft become so solid? Alice's heart pounded. Her pussy tingled at the thought of him pushing it inside of her.

Jack pulled back to remove his pants. Alice went on her knees. She put her hands around his cock again.

"Wait," Jack said removing her hands.

Alice looked up, confused. "I want to pleasure you. To show you I love you."

Jack smiled. "Don't you understand?" He raised her hands so that she would stand. "I get the most pleasure from seeing your pleasure. If you truly love me—" Jack guided her to sit on the bed, "—then you'll let me show you my love."

He bent over to kiss her lips, and cradled her head as he coaxed her to lie down on the bed. Her legs hung over the side of the bed.

Jack caressed the side of her breast as he kissed her. She arched her back into his touch, but his fingers danced around the edges, never touching the tip that yearned for attention.

She broke from his kiss. "Jack, please."

He peered deep into her eyes, shadows playing across his expression of love. As he moved his fingers onto her nipple, she closed her eyes and sighed with delight.

She felt his other hand on her chest. His fingers clutched her breasts, gripping them, kneading them. He plucked and tugged at her nipples. The jolts those hands sent through her body made her hungry for more.

She opened her eyes, Jack looked like he was enjoying her response to his touch.

He nuzzled her neck. Alice gasped. She had no idea kisses there could feel so good. He nibbled her ear, she squealed, his warm mouth arousing her. She throbbed. Alice squeezed her legs together. Lord, she almost had an orgasm just from Jack nibbling her ear!

Jack traced a line of kisses down to a breast, and took the nipple in his mouth, his hot tongue swirling. Alice placed her hands on his head and pushed herself deeper into his mouth. Alice took it all in. How it was to feel Jack's ravenous lips clamp down on her breast. To feel Jack's wet tongue polish her nipple. To feel Jack's hot breath on her skin. To feel Jack. To really feel him.

A part of her wished she had a pillow under her head so she wouldn't have to lift her head to look at Jack. But she didn't dare say anything that might ruin the moment.

She ran her hands through his scruffy hair. Then, from out of nowhere, she had the urge to feel his chin, to feel what the stubs of his facial hair were like.

She lifted her head to look at Jack, reached her hands down and felt the roughness of his chin. Rough and somehow comforting.

Jack looked up at her. She took her hands off his face.

"Is something wrong?" He asked.

She put her hands back on his grizzled chin. "I like the feel of your face," Alice said thinking how stupid that must have sounded.

But Jack smiled and bent down to lavish his wet attention on her other breast.

Alice rested her head. With a low, sensuous moan, she clenched her thighs in anticipation.

Jack replaced his lips with his hands and leaned

up to meet her lips. "I love you, Alice." He kissed her.

All those dreams she had of wanting to hear Jack say those words. All those fantasies of him confessing his love to her. Now it was actually happening.

Hearing his words of love made her dizzy. It was a good thing she was lying down.

Jack hooked the sides of her panties and removed them.

Alice's chest fluttered.

Jack opened her legs. Alice could only see the top half of his head between her thighs. Jack looked back at her. What was that look? It almost looked predatory. Alice's body flushed at his daring glare. He kissed the inside of her thigh. Then kissed the inside of her other thigh. All the while he kept his eyes locked on hers. Jack kissed her first thigh again, closer to her center. Then the other thigh. He made this slow back and forth journey of kisses inching to her core. And it wasn't the kisses that Alice felt were closing in on her. It was that look. That look in his eyes working its way into her very soul. All the locked doors she had previously held shut to protect her, all the impossible doorways, too small for anyone to get through to reach her. Jack was knocking each one down with that look.

Alice's heart thundered.

He was so close.

He suddenly thrust his tongue into her. Alice gasped. *What happened to slow? What happened to gradual?*

Jack's tongue pushed in and out of her, pressing at her inner walls as if to knock those down, too.

Alice moaned, all coherent thoughts gone.

Jack sucked and lavished her folds. She was slick and overflowing with her essence. Her muscles tensed as she felt something build inside her.

Why was Jack being so good to her? Alice barely touched him. Why did he act as though he didn't care about receiving pleasure? He'd said that her own pleasure gave him the most pleasure.

Alice breathed out. If she wanted to please Jack, she needed to let herself fully appreciate his embrace.

Alice felt the roughness of Jack's chin at her pussy, his mouth upon her clit. A flush of heat rippled from between her thighs across her chest and to her face. She cried out. Hands were squeezing her breasts.

Whose hands are those? Alice wondered. *Oh, wait. They're mine.*

His tongue, Jack's tongue, circled around. Like the minute hand on a clock, his tongue traced the hours.

Believe it, Alice told herself. She panted, as Jack's tongue did its magic. She clutched her breasts and pulled her nipples.

Jack's hot licks clocked faster, twirling in hard, slippery laps. Then he slipped a fingertip inside her. Alice bunched the bed covers in her fists, her body tensing, her head lifting off the bed. That finger pushed just through her entrance. Lord, his powerful tongue on her clit!

Believe it, Alice told herself again. *Jack loves you. Believe it.*

Deeper, the finger went. Alice was close. She could feel it. And what was that? Another finger pushing in to join the first!

Alice tossed her head and panted. Oh. My. Lord. Her pussy pulsed around Jack's fingers.

"More!" she moaned.

His fingers pushed deeper into her.

Alice shuddered. *Oh!*

Another finger slipped inside, the three digits pumping into her.

She tensed, inhaled.

Jack licked, rapid, around and around.

She screamed.

His fingers were deep all the way in, wiggling and stroking and touching and playing.

Alice exhaled. "Jack!"

Her stomach tightened and her head lifted off the bed and she shouted out incoherently and she heard her heart pounding in her ears and her pussy clenched around Jack's fingers and she felt herself gush and fireworks exploded in her head and Jack's love electrified her entire body.

And she believed.

Alice panted. She let her head rest on the bed to

catch her breath. She didn't realize how tiring a climax could be. And she didn't even do any of the work!

She was still pulsing around his fingers. Jack kept them inside her and sat beside her on the bed. Alice looked up at his face above her. His chin glistened in the candlelight. Alice caressed his chin. Rough. Wet. Jack kissed her and Alice tasted herself on his lips.

Jack removed his fingers. He climbed on top of her and cradled her head in his hands with a loving embrace. She felt the realness of his full body, his love, solid upon her. His chest on her breasts. His hips on hers. Skin to skin. Heart to heart.

Her arms around him, she wrapped her legs around his torso and squeezed her love for him.

Alice felt Jack against her folds.

He propped himself up on his hands above her and peered into her eyes.

"I've wanted to be inside you for so long," he said.

He reached down and brushed his cock up and down between her folds as he kissed her cheek.

When Alice felt him push his mushroom tip just inside, butterflies fluttered in her belly.

Jack kissed her lips.

A trial. To see how much she could hold. She was stretched. She gasped. She shuddered. He was big. The jury was still out on that one.

He planted his mouth on her breasts, and painted her budding red nipples until they blossomed wet with his tongue.

Now she was ready. She pulled him in deeper, until they were skin upon skin. More! She wanted more!

"Jack, Fill me or I'll go mad!"

Jack raised his head and smiled at Alice. "Your gorgeous when you're mad."

He kissed her.

He filled her.

He held her.

Alice sucked in a deep breath, and bit her lip. Feeling herself stretched wide open like that. Ah, it was so good.

He was inside her. Jack was inside her. She let out a small cry and sucked in another breath. So big. So much of him. Her body trembled with the promise of another orgasm. Alice tried to adjust to his size by moving just a little. She let out another small cry and sucked in a breath. Her pussy squeezed around his cock feeling how wide it stretched her. The sensation was too much. He was touching her sensitive nerves. He was touching her inner walls. He was touching her heart. A wave rumbled in her body demanding that she move again. Alice shifted her hips and let out another cry.

"Jack!" A second orgasm wracked her body.

She wrapped her arms around his chest and held him close.

He held her tenderly. Time drifted.

Alice noticed Jack was getting soft. Jack brushed her cheek.

"I need to move," he said looking in her eyes. "Are you ready?"

Alice nodded. She felt his length pull out and then fill her. Slow strokes. Alice relaxed and let him move within, enjoying the sensations. He was getting harder. Bigger.

Unbelievable. He was with her. Inside her. Jack. Beloved Jack. Feeling that big, beautiful cock of his sliding in and out of her scorching wet pussy, feeling his strong arms holding her tight, feeling his muscular body on top of her own, Alice's body never felt this way before. It wasn't just the sensations. It was more than that. It was the man that was Jack. It was this woman that was Alice. It was the union of them. As one. Together.

Jack thrust faster, his arms tighter around her. The combined scents of his musky cock inside her tart pussy made her head swim. The pounding of his hips on her clit shot powerful bolts of lightning through her body. Her breaths climbed to reach the peak.

And she realized. What they had together, their bond, that's what made her body feel so alive. All that time concentrating on trying to orgasm just got in the way. This whole time, all she really needed was to love. And be loved. And to accept that she could be loved.

"Jack," Alice whispered and arched her back. "I feel you."

Jack took her hand in his. "I have you."

That sent her over the edge. Her body convulsed beneath him, waves of ecstasy washing over her.

Jack cried out and shoved his cock deep inside her, grinding his waist against her wet clit. Those gyrating hips against her nub made those waves of ecstasy turn into a hurricane. She arched her back pressing her electrified nipples into his beefy chest.

He shot his seed into her. "Alice!"

"Yes!" She closed her legs tight around him, thrusting her hips up to meet his. Fire scorched through her body. Her toes curled. Her pussy quaked with spasms as she felt his hot liquid shoot into her. She throbbed around his thick shaft. Her clit pulsed. As the exhilarating storm passed, Jack's love broke through her clouds, shining upon her. Her heart swelled.

No longer insignificant. No longer small. Alice felt big. Beautifully big.

She held Jack. He was still, except for his chest rising and falling.

He caressed her cheek and smiled. "How do you feel?"

She ran her fingertips over his face and stroked the bristles on his chin. "I feel like this is the beginning of a wonderful adventure."

About the Author

Liz Adams, bestselling author of the erotic fairy tale *Alice's Sexual Discovery in a Wonderful Land*, lives in the San Francisco Bay Area, CA. Her short story *Amy "Red" Riding's Hood*, an erotic version of *Red Riding Hood*, is an Amazon bestseller and winner of Goodreads' Book of the Month for October 2012. Her modern day erotic version of Goldilocks, *Goldie's Locks and the Three Men*, is also a bestseller. Liz studied music and creative writing at UCLA and worked as a freelance model before making her writing her career. In her spare time she cuddles with her husband on the couch to watch her favorite shows and often they work together doing hands-on research for her books.

If you enjoyed *Alice's Sexual Discovery*, please write a review on Amazon and/or Goodreads! Also, Liz would love to know how you heard about her book, so drop her a line at LizAdamsBooks@gmail.com or at her website www.LizAdamsAuthor.com.

Also by

Liz Adams

Fairy Tale Erotica
Alice's Erotic Adventures through the Mirror
(Alice's Erotic Adventures Book 2)
If you met your true self, would you recognize her?

Alice's Story of O:
An Erotic Retelling of The Princess and the Pea
(Alice's Erotic Adventures Book 3)
A Choose-Your-Own-Spice Adventure
How taboo are you willing to go?

Goldie's Locks and the Three Men
(A Modern Erotic Fairy Tale Fantasy for Women)
*What if the only way to find the right man
was to instead find the right men?*

Ariel's Super Power of Love
The Erotic Wonders of a Super Heroic Woman
*Ever wonder what Wonder Woman's
love life was like?*

Short Stories
Amy "Red" Riding's Hood
(Fairy Tale Erotica)

Hansel & Gretel and the Sexual Hunter
(A Modern Erotic Fairy Tale)

Alina Said, Call Me Maybe
(A Short Romance)

Short Stories in Anthologies
"Squirting Secrets" in Campus Sexploits 3:
Naughty Tales of Wild Girls in College
(Out of Print!)

"College Sex with a Foreign Exchange Student, the
Universal Language" in *Campus Sexploits 4*
(Out of Print!)

"The Artist" in Sensexual: A Unique Anthology
2013 Vol. 1
(Urban Fantasy)